ENCHANTED
EMPORIUM

D1005736

ENCHANTED EMPORIUM

2

Enchanted Emporium is published by Capstone Young Readers
A Capstone imprint
1710 Roe Crest Drive
North Mankato, Minnesota 56003
www.capstoneyoungreaders.com

First published in the United States in 2015 by Capstone

© 2012 Atlantyca Dreamfarm s.r.l., Italy
© 2014 for this book in English language (Stone Arch Books)
Text by Pierdomenico Baccalario
Editorial project by Atlantyca Dreamfarm S.r.l., Italy
Illustrations by Iacopo Bruno
Original edition published by Edizioni Piemme S.p.A., Italy
Original title: La bussola dei sogni
International Rights (c) Atlantyca S.p.A., Via Leopardi 8 - 20123 Milano - Italia
foreignrights@atlantyca.it - www.atlantyca.com

Cataloging-in-Publication Data is available on the Library of Congress website.
ISBN: 978-1-4342-6517-3 (library binding)
ISBN: 978-1-4342-6520-3 (paperback)
ISBN: 978-1-62370-157-4 (paper-over-board)

Summary: Finley McPhee's life became rather strange once Aiby Lily arrived in
Applecross. But after the Lily family's grand opening of the Enchanted Emporium,
Finley's life becomes even stranger. Sheep disappear from nearby farms. Fish vanish
from the local lakes and streams. The townsfolk claim that the Green Man, a legend
from a Scottish folk tale, is responsible. Is he just an old fable, or a genuine threat? As
the new defender of the Enchanted Emporium, its up to Finley to find out — with a
little help from his inseparable dog, Patches, of course.

Designer: Alison Thiele

Printed in China by Nordica.
0414/CA21400605
032014   008120NORDF14

COMPASS OF DREAMS

by Pierdomenico Baccalario · Illustrations by Iacopo Bruno

capstone
young readers

TABLE OF CONTENTS

Chapter
ONE

BAD NEWS,
A MEAN MAILMAN,
& HIS NEW VAN

After barely a month of work, the post office fired me. Even though Reverend Prospero didn't use the word "fired," and he assured me that I was good at my job, it didn't change the fact that I was no longer the mailman in Applecross.

"Come with me, boy," Reverend Prospero said. He gestured as if politely inviting me inside, but it felt more like he was pushing me along. "Let's go talk to Jules."

Then again, Reverend Prospero wasn't completely aware of his own strength. At almost six feet, six inches tall, he was the kind of man you wouldn't argue with. His wild eyes and loud voice didn't encourage dissent, either.

"Come on, Patches," I told my dog. He immediately bounded after us.

The person we were going to see, Jules, was the real mailman in Applecross — the one I'd been covering for. We delivered letters to all the farms on the mainland, and sometimes even on the islands. Often the addresses were wrong, which meant I'd have to bike all the way to the other side of the bay to deliver them.

Except for the locals, the world didn't seem to have the slightest idea where Applecross was. I can't blame them, though. Applecross is a small village in the northern part of Scotland. There is just one road that leads to us, and on that road there's a sign that reads: *Watch out, danger ahead. Do not drive on this road if you aren't familiar with it.* No, it's not a joke — that sign actually exists.

But that summer, the real danger didn't come from driving on our roads, though that could be fatal near the rocks of Small Peak. And it wasn't even because of all nineteen sharp turns along the way, nor because of the rabbits crossing the road whenever they heard cars coming (no one knows why our rabbits seem to love engines, but they do). It's not even because of the fog that can come so thick so quickly that it blocks your entire view of the road.

So, what was the real danger, you ask?

Jules the mailman.

I'd taken over Jules's mail route that summer because he twisted his ankle while riding his bicycle. He didn't get a lot of sympathy for his injury because, well . . . he's a cranky guy. And lazy. Case in point: in the four weeks I covered for him, I delivered more mail than he had in the previous six months.

Upon hearing this fact, Jules was predictably angry. "What do you think you're doing, boy?!" he cried. "You're ruining my big plan!"

"And what's your big plan?" I asked.

Jules didn't answer my question. Instead, he got even crankier and swore that he'd make me pay for what I'd done (whatever that was). Then Jules limped out of the post office (he only limped when he was angry) and went to complain to Reverend Prospero, just like everyone else in Applecross did when they had a problem. And as usual, Reverend Prospero found a way to solve the problem — which was why the two of us were talking that day.

"So what do you think?" asked the reverend. He pointed at a red van just outside the post office. It had the Royal Mail's insignia on its side. "Modern technology has finally come to our village."

"You're kidding, right?" I asked.

The reverend continued speaking as if he hadn't heard me. "The central office just sent the van to us," he continued. "Isn't it a beauty?"

I laughed. "Who's supposed to drive it?" I asked sarcastically. "Jules?"

The reverend raised an eyebrow. "And why not?" he asked. "He's the mailman, after all."

The red van looked like a cross between a toaster oven and a death trap. I shivered at the thought of that thing speeding down the roads in Applecross or Belanch Ba, the oxen road, with Jules at the wheel.

"Jules can't drive . . ." I mumbled.

"Neither can you," the reverend pointed out. Which wasn't true at all. I was sure I could drive — it's just that it was illegal since I was only fourteen years old. "Which, I'm afraid, means you're out of a job, boy."

I grumbled and handed over the mailbag. "As you wish," I said. "But don't say I didn't warn you." I paused. "Can I at least keep the bike?"

The reverend didn't even look at me, seemingly entranced by the sparkle of the shiny, red van.

"I have to find a new job for you," he said. "Let's meet again tomorrow morning at my house, boy."

He never seemed to use my name. "My name's Finley McPhee, you know," I said. "With an 'F.'"

The reverend just grumbled and kept his eyes on the van.

"Come on, Patches," I mumbled. "We're leaving."

Getting fired was kind of a bummer, I'll admit it. But thankfully I had a pretty good backup plan for that afternoon . . .

Chapter TWO

UNEMPLOYMENT, THROWING STONES, & TOTAL PANIC

I spent the rest of the morning gathering rocks, then throwing them at a sign hanging from the high-voltage power lines. Patches ran to get the rock every time I threw one, but he didn't bring them back. Patches played by his own rules.

After a couple of hours, the sign finally detached from the lines and fell, splatting in the mud below. Even though it was summer and it hadn't rained much, the mud still came up to my knees. Luckily, I'm Scottish and therefore immune to mud.

I plodded over, dragging my feet through the muck. There was a lightning bolt on the sign. The words beneath it were: *HIGH VOLTAGE — FATAL IF TOUCHED.*

Patches whimpered, meaning he wanted to see it too. So I went back to get him, held him above the mud, and slogged back toward the sign. I held him close to the sign so he could sniff it.

"What do you think, Patches?" I asked. "Do you like it? Maybe we can put it at the entrance to Applecross. Or maybe write Jules's name on it, or the license plate number of the post office's new van."

Patches tilted his head at me, which meant he agreed. "We have to do it this afternoon, then," I said. Whatever new job Reverend Prospero had in mind for me would probably prevent me from doing it tomorrow.

After failing nearly all my classes in school last year, my dad and the reverend agreed that I should spend the summer working. I guess they both hoped that I would absolutely hate it and end up begging to go back to school after summer break was over. Luckily, the Lily family had arrived and opened the Enchanted Emporium. Before then, Applecross was just a sleepy fishing town, and my dad and the reverend would have been right. But since the Lily family arrived, the town's been turned upside-down.

I heard my stomach rumble. "Guess it's time for lunch," I told Patches, and began to trudge my way out of the mud.

The Greenlock Pub was the only place to eat within fifteen miles. Thankfully, the food there was great. Past Greenlock Pub was the McStay Inn. Their food was . . . not great. Past that was the Tourist Information Office, where Blind Jacky worked. He wasn't friendly, although he loved to tell stories to visitors — like when a giant, silvery fish jumped into his boat and tried to eat his eyeballs. Tourists didn't tend to linger long in the Tourist Information Office.

There wasn't much else to do in Applecross. There was a small square, a small church, a parsonage, one souvenir store owned by Mr. Everett (also known as The Professor), one school, Meb's dress shop, and few other buildings. Then there were all the farms in the countryside and along the coastline. Oh, and the sheep. Sheep were everywhere in Applecross. And all they did was eat grass and complain about the weather.

At least with Aiby Lily's arrival, things actually started happening in Applecross. Oh, and she's beautiful. A little bit taller than me, sure, but still really pretty.

Patches whimpered. I saw a shadow appear near my bike. I looked up to see a tall, thin man with hair so blonde it almost looked white. He had an oval-shaped face, and his nose was long and big. He wore a fancy orange cape and a pair of aviator goggles. His hands were long and thin and they were holding an ornately carved cane.

He was Locan Lily, Aiby's father. And seeing him appear out of the blue like that was always a bad sign. The cane he held was called The Trip Stick and it was one of the many magical objects that the Lily family kept safe at their store.

I quietly dropped the sign behind my back. "Good morning, Mr. Lily," I said, wearing my most innocent smile.

Locan Lily scared me a little. Maybe it was because he was very tall, had weird hair, or the fact that he just didn't talk much. I always felt nervous around him, like I'd just walked through his living room in my muddy shoes.

"Is Aiby with you?" he asked, anxious as always.

"No, I haven't seen her today," I said. "Actually . . ."

"Actually?" Mr. Lily repeated, narrowing his eyes.

"I haven't seen her in over a week," I said.

"And you don't know where she is?" he asked.

I shook my head. "Sorry, Mr. Lily."

"Curses," he said.

He stared out into the distance.

"Is there a problem?" I asked.

"Yes. Adele Babele will be here in less than one hour

and we're missing a bookmark," he said casually, as if I had any idea what he was talking about. "A Flower of Vertigo."

"I see," I said and nodded. You see, it was never a good idea to look shocked or curious with the Lily family members. And you definitely didn't want to ask questions. Both Aiby and her father were pretty eccentric. Then again, owners of a store that sold talking swords, charmed rings, magical beans, and stuff like that probably had to be a little weird.

A light breeze blew by that made Locan's white-blonde hair stick up. Annoyed, he tried to smooth it back into place, but didn't have much luck.

"Maybe I can help you?" I said and immediately wished I hadn't.

Locan shrugged. "Maybe you can," he said. "Do you have your key with you?"

I silently cursed my brother Doug for giving me a necklace for the key. He always said that girls loved boys who wore necklaces. My brother wasn't too bright, but that didn't stop girls from being obsessed with him and his rugby games, so I'd taken his advice.

With a sigh, I lifted the necklace out from beneath my shirt. The breeze seemed to grow colder as I held it up.

Mr. Lily looked around suspiciously. Patches started to paw at the dirt. More wind came and it started to bend the trees. The high-voltage cables squeaked.

"We should probably be on our way," Mr. Lily said, pulling me in close. He raised the Trip Stick in front of him. I grabbed hold. Patches sat on my feet.

Mr. Lily pulled a small object out from a hidden pocket inside his cape. It looked like a weird little silk ladder. He held it out in front of him and the ladder started to grow bigger.

"Let's go get that flower!" he said.

"I'm sorry, go where and get what?"

As an answer, Mr. Lily folded the Silky Ladder around my waist and grabbed my wrist tightly.

Mr. Lily yelled a strange word, then beat the Trip Stick on the ground. Our surroundings gave way to complete darkness. Then I realized we were falling.

Mr. Lily was flipping head over heels in a circular motion as he fell through the darkness. "Not again!" he yelled.

I screamed and Patches dug his teeth into my pants as the three of us fell together.

SUBJECTS	MARKS—E (90 % – 100	THE
READING		
COMPOSITION		
DICTATION		
GRAMMAR		
ARITHMETIC		
MENTAL ARITH.		
ATTENDANCE—Possible - Actual -		
Pupil's Name		
N.B.—The Head to intervi children's		

SILKY STAIRCASE

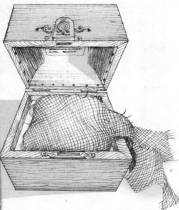

The magical object is so light and slender that it can be held in the palm of your hand. It was woven by Rapunzel in seven days and seven nights using silk produced by enchanted silkworms. The weaving was interrupted, so the Silky Staircase has an unraveled edge that needs to be repaired. If only James Fry's hook could be found...

Chapter
THREE

VERTIGO,
HIGH WALLS,
& FALLS

The weirdest thing was that, while I was falling, I thought about my bike. I'd left it in the grass, near the power lines, without even locking it up. It might seem stupid to worry about a bike while you're presumably falling to your death, but I couldn't help myself.

Then things got even weirder: when I closed my eyes, I could actually see what was happening back in Applecross! The wind had stopped blowing. A man appeared from behind the trees and he slowly walked toward my bike. He gathered the high voltage sign that I'd dropped when Locan had grabbed my wrist. The man absentmindedly slipped the sign into an inside pocket of this really odd, mirror-covered cloak he wore. Then he

put on some headphones, turned up the volume, and left the way he'd come.

BOING! My eyes shot open again as the Silky Staircase strained like a rubber band. I felt myself being pulled by the belt so hard that I could barely breathe. A moment later, I found myself hanging upside down. I watched as some spare change fell from my pockets. Patches was hanging from my shirt by his teeth with his tail wagging furiously in front of my nose. It was not a pleasant sight.

I tried to reach out and grab something to get my balance back only to find I was swimming in the air with nothing to grasp. "What the heck is going on?!" I cried, trying my best not to vomit. Patches wiggled his tail even faster.

"Don't move, you two!" Mr. Lily yelled at us from a few feet above. (Or was he below me?)

Unfortunately I couldn't follow his advice. You see, I'm a little afraid of heights, so I began to flail like a madman. Somehow I found a handhold and I grabbed it. I pulled myself to what I thought was an upright position. Suddenly, the feeling of vertigo forced my eyes shut. Patches released my shirt and attached himself to my belt with his teeth and sat there, growling and barking at the same time.

I realized we were hanging from a rock wall. It was

so tall that it disappeared into the clouds far above us. When I looked down, I saw that I couldn't even see the ground. I had a quick vision of a waterfall, then I heard some strange bird singing.

I held on to the rock even tighter and looked up. Aiby's father was hanging from the wall in a similar fashion about a hundred feet higher.

"Where are we, Mr. Lily?" I yelled, hugging the rock wall as tightly as I could.

Mr. Lily reached beneath his cape and produced a black notepad. The book was surprisingly large, but somehow he managed to flip through the pages with one hand. "Well, if I'm not mistaken . . ."

"Mr. Lily, I really don't want to die like this!" I cried.

"Oh, relax," Mr. Lily said. "A little fresh air won't hurt you. On the contrary, it's quite good for you."

"Fresh air?!" I yelled. "I'm not worried about the air — I'm worried about falling to my death! And how can you call this fresh air? It's freezing!"

"It's just the altitude," Mr. Lily said, ignoring all but the least important part of my statement. "Slow your breathing or you'll use up all your oxygen."

I couldn't decide if I was more angry or scared. "Just tell me why we're hundreds of miles above the ground!" I begged.

"Because this is the only place where we can find a Flower of Vertigo," Mr. Lily said as if nothing was strange about the scenario.

"You're insane!" I yelled.

In the meantime Patches dug his nails into my jeans.

Locan Lily read from his book: "*The Imaginary Travelers* limited edition guide tells us that we should follow the Mallory rope line. It's supposed to be somewhere around — OUCH!"

I saw the large book fall from Mr. Lily's hands, zip past me, and then disappear below.

"Did you grab it?" Mr. Lily asked me.

"Are you seriously asking me if I grabbed a giant book that you dropped from a hundred feet above me?" I said. "Did you really just ask me that?!" I laughed at the idea that Mr. Lily thought it would be possible to let go of the rock and catch a falling book that size with one hand. "Of course I didn't grab it!"

"This is a problem," Mr. Lily said.

"Why?" I cried. "Why is this a problem?!"

"When Aiby finds out that I lost it, she will be very upset," he said.

"Aiby will be angry you lost a book?!" I cried in disbelief. "We're hanging from a ladder made of —"

I looked up to examine the ladder and realized

that the ladder was simply floating in midair. "IT'S HANGING FROM NOTHING!" I howled.

Mr. Lily put on his aviator goggles. A sparkle appeared on the brass frame. "It's a Silky Staircase," he said in an annoyed tone. "It stands up on its own without being attached to anything. Also, if you pull it twice . . ."

He yanked it twice. The staircase tensed, then immediately dropped me about two hundred feet.

"DON'T EVER DO THAT AGAIN!" I cried. Desperately, I tried to dig my fingers into a crack in the rock. I crammed them in and braced my ribs against the wall. As I wiggled my fingers farther inside, I felt something brush against them.

I glanced inside the crack and discovered a ring. I blinked hard, then looked at it again. There was definitely an iron ring inside the rock.

"There's a ring here!" I yelled. "I found a ring!"

"What type of ring?" Mr. Lily called back.

"I don't know!" I moved my free foot to explore the rock below me. "And there's another one below it!"

"Oh, good!" Mr. Lily yelled. "Then we're in the right place. That has to be George Mallory's climbing trail!"

"Who's George Mallory?" I yelled.

"The British hiker who first put these climbing rings here!" he yelled. "He was the first man to ever climb

Mount Everest, but he never climbed back down the mountain."

I grabbed onto the rock even tighter. "That's fascinating, Mr. Lily," I snapped. "But what about *us*?!"

"The good news is," Mr. Lily said, "we must be close to the Flower of Vertigo! Look around for it, boy!"

"What does it look like?" I asked.

"It's a blue flower that's a little bit bigger than a penny."

I glanced around. "And if I find one, can we go back home?" I asked.

"Yes, so start looking!"

But there was nothing to see besides clouds and rocks. And the rings left by that British hiker. Mr. Lily searched the rock near him with his hands. He was moving cautiously, one foot at a time, one arm at a time. I got vertigo just watching him.

I tried to move, but everything was more difficult with Patches hanging from me. I crab-walked to the right where I hoped to find more rings. As I inched along, I thought of a bunch of good deeds I would do if I managed to get out of this situation alive. I had a lot to make up for, to be honest. I mean, I'd thrown stones at signs and pestered Aiby about the Enchanted Emporium's secrets. I endlessly mocked Doug about the smell of his aftershave. I'd even lied to my dad and said I'd fed the sheep when it was raining. And yeah, skipping school to go fishing for an entire semester was probably the worst thing I'd done that year.

As I squirmed across the wall looking for this stupid blue flower, I tried to convince myself that this situation wasn't so weird after all. Thinking of all the weird things that had happened to me since I first met the Lilys kept me grounded. I'd been kidnapped by a raving Dutchman who spoke an absurd language. I'd fought a stone giant using the powers of an ancient Scottish hero — and then defeated him in a game of riddles.

When I really thought about it, climbing a sky-high wall wasn't all that tall of a tale.

Patches, now with his teeth clenched into my belt, started to wiggle furiously. "What's wrong, Patches?" I asked, looking down. Once again, I got struck by vertigo and I felt a knot tighten in my stomach.

"What's up, boy?" I said, fighting back the urge to vomit. My dog just kept wiggling.

"Patches," I said. "Please stay still . . ."

But he wouldn't listen. All of a sudden, my belt went loose . . . and so did my pants.

"PAAAATCHES!" I yelled, feeling the cold mountain wind sting my butt. I was quick enough to pinch my feet

together and catch my pants — and my dog — before they fell to their doom.

Patches continued to wiggle. "Are you trying to get us both killed, Patches?!" I yelled at my dog. That's when I saw them.

"Mr. Lily!" I cried.

"What?" Mr. Lily yelled back.

"I found those flowers!" I cried. "Actually, Patches found them!"

"Where are they?"

"Down here, a few feet below me!"

"What the heck happened to your pants?"

"My dog did it," I said, immediately realizing how silly that sounded. "Can you see Patches, Mr. Lily?"

"Yes . . ."

"Well, the flowers you're looking for are right next to him!"

"Are you positive?"

"Yes."

"Then let go!"

"Let go what?"

"Let go of the rock!"

"MR. LILY I CAN'T!"

"JUST DO IT!"

Mr. Lily yanked the Silky Staircase twice. It loosened

and made him fall. But I stayed right where I was, holding onto the rock, as Mr. Lily fell right past me. When the staircase tensed again, he was right below me, next to Patches.

"My dog is falling, Mr. Lily!"

"You're right!" he chirped. "It's the Flower of Vertigo!"

I clenched my teeth in frustration. I was about to yell at Mr. Lily when I felt my shoes start to slip off my feet. Patches barked and tried to jump on Mr. Lily's head.

"Got it!" Mr. Lily said, plucking a blue, penny-sized flower.

"MR. LILY!" I howled. "DO SOMETHING!"

He looked at me through his big goggles and smiled like everything was right in the world. "I told you to let go of it."

"No way!" I said.

"Then you'll have to stay here," Mr. Lily said. He placed the Flower of Vertigo in a pocket inside his cape, then picked another one. "The Trip Stick only works if you beat it on the ground, you know."

My eyes went wide. "But the ground is miles below us."

Mr. Lily smiled. "Correct."

My shoe fell off my foot, followed by my jeans. Patches barked and landed on Mr. Lily's shoulder.

"Just pretend you're the greatest magical bungee jumper in the whole world," Mr. Lily said. His enthusiasm made me furious.

I didn't want to go bungee jumping — whether it was magical or not. But I didn't seem to have any other options.

"One!" Mr. Lily said. "Two!"

For some reason, I started laughing.

"Three! LET GO!" he cried.

I closed my eyes and pushed myself away from the wall. I felt weightless and very cold. The wind howled, Patches barked, and then Mr. Lily yelled a strange word:

Then I passed out.

FLOWERS, EMOSSIFICATION, & ADELE BABELE

"I'm dead," I said. I spoke calmly and with the dignity of acceptance. After all, I was surprised to have made it this far after meeting Aiby's dad.

I opened my eyes to see a blurry, red surface above me. It seemed an odd color for the afterlife. I blinked once, then twice, but the red surface stayed right where it was. I couldn't feel my body. Rather, I felt like I was surrounded by cottony clouds. Floating.

It reminded me of one of those boring philosophical movies that Doug used to watch so he'd have something to talk to girls about. One of them claimed the soul weighs twenty-one grams. Considering the fuzzy way I felt, that sounded about right.

"Yeah," I mumbled deliriously. "I only weigh twenty-one grams now."

Suddenly Aiby Lily's face appeared above me with one eyebrow raised. "McPhee, what are you mumbling about?" she said.

I lurched upright. "Where am I?!"

Aiby didn't answer right away. "Where do you think you are?" she finally asked.

I looked around to find I was sitting on a couch in a living room with a red ceiling. There was a big carpet beneath the couch. A furry shape rested on the floor.

"Patches!" I cried.

Aiby smiled. "He ate everything I had in the kitchen and then stayed by your side for two straight hours," she said. "Hungry and loyal — like owner, like dog, I guess."

She put one hand on my shoulder. Our eyes met. *Oh man*, I thought. *She's so beautiful. I could handle being dead if she were my guardian angel.*

Aiby sighed and stood up. She was wearing a white and blue striped tank top over an orange and green t-shirt. As usual, she looked really weird, but also elegant.

"My dad is in the lab mixing the Flowers of Vertigo with the Gardener of Pages," Aiby said, breaking the silence.

I nodded. That meant I could only be in the Enchanted

Emporium. I rubbed my eyes, taking in all the details around me. The small living room was filled to the brim with shelves of books. The shelves were painted red, just like the floor and ceiling. There was a wide variety of multi-colored books. In fact, there were weird objects all over the place. I spotted a little stuffed elephant with buttons for eyes, a silver bag with smoke billowing from it, a crystal submarine, a tin soldier that marched from one side of the room to the other, and an unsettling painting of an old lady who yawned or made faces when you looked at her.

Patches was sleeping on Sinbad the Sailor's Flying Carpet. He seemed to enjoy the fact that he was hovering a foot above the ground. Underneath the only window in the room, I saw a small desk with a huge book, a self-typing typewriter, and an opened suitcase that looked very familiar. There was something new about it, though: inside were two sparkling eyes and a pirate's sword. I shivered.

"When you're ready, come into the lab in the back," Aiby said. "I'm waiting for an important client."

"Where were you this morning?" I asked.

Aiby ignored me and crossed the room. She peered between the curtains. "Dad!" she said. "How's the Herbarium and the Flower of Vertigo coming together?"

Even though I still had no idea what the Flower of Vertigo, Gardener of the Pages, and the Herbarium were, I could tell it wasn't the right time to ask. After all, Aiby was waiting on an important client. And ignoring my questions, as usual.

"Wait, Aiby," I said. "I'll come with you."

I leapt up from the couch. It was only then that I remembered I didn't have pants on. I turned bright red and immediately dove back underneath the blanket.

Aiby giggled. "I left you a pair of my dad's pants on the side of the couch," she said.

She walked over to the desk where a big book lay. When she opened it, a soft trumpeting and golden light filled the room. "Dad!" she yelled, clearly upset. "How many times do I have to tell you not to leave the Flowers of Fame between the pages of great-grandpa's book?!"

I used the distraction to slip on my new pair of pants while staying beneath the blanket. Thankfully, the pants were my size. They were nice, too, with smooth fabric and big pockets on the sides. While I was buttoning them, Aiby took a dried flower from between the pages of the book she referred to as her great-grandfather's. It was wrapped in a silver net.

"This is it," she whispered. She carefully placed it between the pages of another nearby book.

Without disturbing Patches, I walked over to Aiby. She quickly flipped through some pages written in an alphabet with letters that actually moved. I recognized it as the Enchanted Language, a secret and magical alphabet. That also meant that the large tome must be *The Big Book of Magical Objects*, which was the most important of all the relics kept in the Enchanted Emporium.

Aiby was standing stiffly like she always does when she's upset. "What are you looking for?" I asked quietly.

"I'm checking to see if we're using this Herbarium correctly," she said.

"Oh," I said, following the movement of her finger through the pages. The letters of the Enchanted Language shifted before my eyes. I thought I recognized some of the words among the lines, but couldn't be sure.

"How are you doing with the Enchanted Language?" she asked me.

"Oh, pretty good," I lied. I had studied the language a little bit in my free time, but I still struggled to understand it. Then again, I struggled with all foreign languages, but the Enchanted Language was definitely the toughest.

"I'm still having trouble with some of the letters." That was a bit of an understatement considering the

only words I could read so far were "chase," "stomp," and "taste." Oh, and "book." I think.

I glanced at the picture on the other side of the page. It showed a small metal robot holding a flower in one hand and an open book in the other. The drawing seemed to suggest that the flower was supposed to be placed inside a certain page of the robot's book.

I opened the other book where Aiby had placed the dry flower a second before. Once again, trumpeting and golden light filled the air.

"Flower of Fame?" I asked, immediately closing the book.

"Yes," Aiby said. "The Gardener of Pages explains how to plant the flower among the pages of the book, then the emossification process begins."

I raised an eyebrow. "Huh?"

"Emossification is the drying of the emotions of the flower," Aiby said. "It's done this way to distill the flower's characteristics and grant them to the book. The technique was discovered by the botanists Hyeronimus Bock and Otto Brunfels when they created the collection of Laquedem, the librarian's talking books." Aiby flipped through the pages. "Now where is it . . . Grasslight, Flower of Opera, Scent of Sun . . . ah, here it is! Flower of Vertigo, used for books that are short of breath!"

Yeah, Aiby's a little weird.

"Dad!" she yelled, making Patches jump. She immediately closed *The Big Book of Magical Objects* and entered the lab. I heard her nervously telling her dad that the book said they needed at least five days to emossify a Flower of Vertigo. "And Adele Babele is coming today!"

I put my hand on the book cover. It was thick and well worn. Beneath my fingers, a tiny light gleamed. It was like the pages of *The Big Book of Magical Objects* could feel my presence. A voice in my head told me to let go, but I ignored it and read the ex libris, or bookplate on the first page. It wasn't written in the Enchanted Language, but in Latin, in pale ink.

Diamond Lily

The Big Book of Magical Objects

868 A.D.

It seemed impossible to me that the book could be that old. Then again, Aiby once told me that her ancestors created the book centuries before the invention of print. I tried to get a better look when I realized that the letters were floating above the actual page.

I quickly slammed the book shut. Then I wandered aimlessly around the room like I usually did whenever I was inside the Enchanted Emporium. I didn't want to

touch anything for fear that it might attack me, explode, or who knows what else.

I stopped in front of a shelf of books and put one hand in my pants pocket. As soon as my fingers slipped inside, I felt something grab them.

"What's that?!" I cried. I tried to free myself, but my hand was definitely being grasped by another hand.

"AIBY!" I yelled. "Aiby, there's something inside these pants!"

I heard her bare feet slap against the hardwood floor as she came running. "What's wrong, Finley?"

I pointed at my trapped arm and held the elbow out. "I'm stuck!" I said.

Aiby slapped her forehead. "Oh, right! I forgot! Sorry!" she said quickly. "We'll get you free in a second."

"Free from what, Aiby?!" I cried.

"It's called a Dark Pocket. It's used by people who need to carry around a bunch of things that wouldn't fit in a normal pocket." Aiby glanced toward the window. "Just a second, my customer has arrived!"

The dream-catcher at the entrance door of the Enchanted Emporium chimed as the door opened.

"Oh, no you don't, Aiby!" I said. "You can't leave me like this!"

Just then, a large lady wrapped in layers of veils and

black lace entered the Emporium. Her face was pale and covered with a thick layer of makeup. Her hair was made into a big bun that reminded me of a sombrero. She had an intense scent wafting around her that was pleasant and disgusting at the same time.

I hid behind a wall, making sure no one could see me. I'd never witnessed a business transaction at the Enchanted Emporium before, so I didn't know what to expect.

As I peeked out, I saw Aiby give a tiny bow. "Welcome in our humble store, Madame Babele," she said.

"Oh, it's the young Lily daughter!" Madame Babele said. The scents of apple pie and rotting garbage filled my nostrils. "What a nice surprise to see you working here! My dear, you look exactly like your mother."

Mr. Lily appeared behind his daughter. "Um, Welcome, Adele," he said. He was still wearing his aviator goggles. "Good to see you found your way here."

"It was an easy trip!" she boomed. "I never travel without my Suitcase of Stars, and it never sends me to the wrong place. Speaking of places, you've got yourselves a really nice shop here! Reginald always had good taste as far as locations are concerned. Very peaceful and quiet."

You wouldn't say that if you'd been here when the stone giant was rampaging around, I thought.

The lady set her tattered suitcase on the counter. I immediately recognized it, but couldn't remember from where . . .

"Yes, Reginald clearly had a knack for locations," Adele continued. "And he definitely had a knack for finding books!" She chuckled. "You wonderful Lilys."

"At your service, Madame Babele," said Aiby. "As is our endless library of magical books."

"Sadly, I can't read the Enchanted Language as well as I used to," she said. "Which is why I came here to buy more dried flowers."

Mr. Lily retrieved an object from underneath the counter. It looked somewhat like a shoe box. He opened it and peered inside. A look of disgust grew on his face. "I'm sorry to say this, Adele, but none of your old flowers can be replaced or fixed . . ."

"Oh?" she said flatly. "What a shame . . ."

Mr. Lily lifted a few silver nets with flowers inside them. As he did, they broke into pieces. "You really need to stop putting them inside books written in dead languages. They require fresh air at least every twenty years, or they end up dead, too."

"I forget, Locan. I forget!" she said.

Aiby's dad smiled. "And if you forget, you lose," he said.

The big lady seemed to be getting even bigger. She seemed to be inhaling but not exhaling. "That's the way it is," she said. I caught the scent of banana mingled with rotten fish. "So what do we do now?"

Aiby lined up some dried flowers on the counter. "We managed to prepare four Happy Flowers, one Remember Me Not, ten Flowers of Boredom, and the same amount of Health Flowers."

Adele Babele nodded. "A name for every flower."

"As for the Flower of Vertigo, you'll have to wait another five days," Mr. Lily added.

"Five days?" she asked.

"That is the amount of time the Gardener needs to prepare the emossification," Mr. Lily explained.

"Five days, Locan? That's an unbearably long time to wait!"

"We could always send you the flower inside a book," Aiby offered.

"But which book, my dear? Do you have a book I don't yet possess? I find that hard to believe, as I have almost all the books in the entire world!" She laughed, shaking her veils. "Actually, now that I think about it, there is one book I'd like to have!"

"*The Big Book of Magical Objects* is not for sale, Adele," Mr. Lily immediately replied.

She made a sour face. "Maybe it will be available soon. After all, people are saying that change is on the horizon. You know, that the old stores don't exist anymore."

"Who says that?" Mr. Lily asked.

"Rumors from other families," she said flatly. "I'm surprised you Lilys don't know about this. There's a colleague of yours who wants to open the shop to everyone, maybe even sell to department stores . . ."

"Not a chance," Mr. Lily said. "We'd rather be dead than let the Enchanted Emporium break from our tradition of discretion, Adele."

"But sales are so bad that business is almost dead already," she said. "Am I right?"

Mr. Lily blushed. I saw a glint of anger flash in his eyes, but he kept himself under control. "Better to be almost dead than almost alive."

Just then, I noticed that a couple of multicolored cockroaches were falling from Adele's huge hair bun. They scurried down her legs, then hid between the floorboards.

"We can give you a big discount on your purchase," Aiby said, returning to the business at hand. "And if we can't find a safe way to have the flower delivered to you, you can get it yourself next time you visit."

Adele Babele turned to look at Aiby. Adele's big, white face was as pale as the moon and her cold eyes looked like two pieces of jade.

"A big discount, Miss Lily?!" she cried. "Do you hear your daughter, Locan? She has a better business sense than you do!"

Adele Babele reached to grab the other flowers with her ring-covered fingers. Aiby grabbed them first, saying, "Advance payment, please. In gold, of course."

THE TIN SOLDIER

This magical object belonged to a small army that invaded the tiny country of Andorra in the Pyrenees Mountains in 1278. The soldiers arrived by sea, courtesy of Captain Lemuel Gulliver, who left them with a map and an unspecified mission. After conquering Andorra, the army was scattered to the four winds. These brave soldiers are commemorated in one of Hans Christian Andersen's famous stories.

Chapter
FIVE

FRAUNANKEN!
MURZEN!
VAZ!

As soon as Adele Babele had left, Mr. Lily opened all the Enchanted Emporium's windows to get rid of the horrible smell she'd left behind.

"Coming back later to get the Flower of Vertigo, is she?!" Mr. Lily growled. "We should ban her from the store — permanently!"

Outside, on the chalk-white cliffs, a flock of seagulls seemed to be following Madame Babele's carriage. *That's weird,* I thought.

Aiby sat down on the counter and swung her long legs back and forth. "We don't have enough clients anymore to be banning customers, Dad," she said.

"We're making ends meet," Mr. Lily muttered.

"And what happens if we can't make ends meet?" Aiby asked.

"Everything will be lost," he answered. "Magical objects, spells, enchanted books . . . *poof* — all gone! But that's the way the world goes. Everything eventually comes to an end." He sighed, then left the room.

From the way they had been talking, I got the feeling Aiby had forgotten I was there. I felt like a spy. Whenever I'd asked Aiby about magical objects disappearing before, she'd just told me that the last maker of magical objects had been killed in 1789 during the so-called "Enlightenment Revolution." But beyond that, Aiby wasn't willing to talk about it.

"Hey, Aiby," I said, reminding her I was still there. "Tough client, huh?"

Aiby turned to look at me. I was right — she had forgotten I was there. I tried to smile at her, but the hand inside my pocket pulling my hand was hard to ignore.

Aiby rested her face in her hands. "No tougher than other customers," she said.

"But everything turned out fine in the end, right?" I asked.

"We sold plenty of stock and probably retained an important client," Aiby said. "So, yes, I suppose everything went okay. Thanks for going out with my dad this morning to search for the Flower of Vertigo, by the way."

"Oh, sure. It was no problem at all," I said. After all, I'd only nearly fallen to my death three times. "We should thank Patches instead, though. He found the flowers."

"Yeah, the flowers," mumbled Aiby. "We've known we needed them for a week. I kept telling dad to remember to get them for the Gardener of Pages, but he seemed like he had something more important to do."

"I understand," I lied. Truth was, my own dad never had something more important to do. He just did one thing: take care of the farm. Well, he also complained about the weather every other day.

"Do you want to see it?" Aiby asked. "The Gardener of Pages, I mean."

I was more interested in solving the problem of my hand trapped inside my pocket, but I couldn't say no to her. "Oh yes. Sure."

She jumped off the counter and led me to one of the other rooms in the shop. Once again I was surprised how much bigger the house was than it looked. From the outside, it seemed like a simple, small, red house. But once inside, the small space was filled with seemingly endless rooms that looked like they were constantly changing positions. I couldn't shake the feeling that, if I weren't following Aiby, I would've gotten lost. We passed through a small kitchen with a weird pan boiling on an old stove. From there we went underneath a wooden staircase and into Locan's lab.

It was a dark room in a corner of the house with no windows. It looked like a mix between a carpenter's shop and an alchemist's toilet: there were saws and hammers hanging on the walls, vases, funnels, stills, syringes, and countless candles of different colors on every surface.

"There it is," said Aiby. "The Gardener of Pages. We call him Hyeronimus Bock."

At first glance, the so-called Gardener of Pages looked like a small child sitting on a table. As I got closer, I saw it was actually a mechanical dwarf made of wood and metal. It had a big grin, red cheeks, and velvet overalls that went just past his knees.

Without warning, its head tilted and its mouth opened. "Fraunanken!" it said. "Fuzzlabein! Frallich von Halles!"

I jumped in surprise. "Is it . . . broken?"

"I can't understand him," Aiby said with a shrug. She placed one hand on the Gardener's back. "He's been talking this way since we recharged him, but we can't fix him since we don't have the instructions."

"Murzen! Hopper, hopper! Vaz!" said the dwarf.

"It sounds German," I said.

"German, Dutch . . . there's a bit of everything in there," said Aiby. "As soon as he loses his charge, we're going to have to find a way to fix him. Maybe Meb knows how."

Meb was Applecross's dressmaker, but she'd also been chosen as the official repair person for the Enchanted Emporium. She was a young woman with a friendly smile who was gifted at fixing things, especially relationships between people.

"Are you sure?" I asked. I glanced suspiciously at the Gardener. "What do you think, little fella?"

"Flock! Dun Grunz!" it said.

We both laughed.

"Listen, Aiby," I said, trying to lift my trapped arm. "I don't want to annoy you, but I'm having a wardrobe malfunction . . ."

"Are you really studying the Enchanted Language, Finley?" she said instead of answering me.

"What?" I asked.

"Are you really trying to learn the Enchanted Language?" she asked. "Are you just joking when you say you'll never learn it?"

If there was one thing I was terrible at, it was learning

languages. I must have had some kind of sickness, or maybe an allergy, because I couldn't remember a single rule of grammar or anything like that. Even Welsh and Southern English were tricky for me.

"Oh," I mumbled. "Let's just say I'm making progress. Of course, it's taking me forever, but I have lots of other stuff to do too. Did I tell you that they fired me from my mail route?"

"No. And what will you do to make money now?" she said while digging through the papers on her dad's desk.

"Fraaatz! Wragger!" the Gardener of Pages said.

"I have no idea," I said. "But hopefully Reverend Prospero does."

Aiby handed me a label. At the top was a coat of arms depicting a tree with gemstones as fruit. Below that was an inscription:

SCARSELLI FAMILY
THE MAGNIFICENT ONES
Florence – Buenos Aires
Since 1571

On the back, there were ten lines written in the Enchanted Language that I couldn't read.

"Why did you give me this?" I asked her.

"It's the instructions for how to get your hand out of your pants," Aiby said.

"Listen, I don't have time for this," I said. "Can you please just help me out?"

"Really, Finley?" Aiby said. "I've been begging and pleading for you to learn to read the Enchanted Language for three weeks. Three whole weeks!"

"I've been trying!" I insisted.

"Well keep trying! And free yourself."

I waved the label with my free hand. "But this is ten lines of text! I'm not that good yet!"

"If I hadn't known you before now, Finley," Aiby said, "I'd think you were as dumb as a rock."

"I think you're confusing me with my brother," I said.

"Oh, really!" Aiby said, then she bit her lip. She seemed like she wanted to tell me something.

I tried to explain once again that I was practicing every night with the vocabulary she'd given me, but the letters still looked weird. Aiby just stared at me and listened. I felt like I was back in school again, and she was one of my teachers.

I tried to change the subject. "I have to go get my bike and head home," I said. "Otherwise my parents will start to worry about me."

Aiby smiled. It was so beautiful and cold at the same time. "It'll be tough to ride a bike with just one hand . . ."

"So you'll help me, then?" I asked.

Careful what you're asking, a voice in the back of my head suggested.

"Not a chance," Aiby said.

"What? Why not?! That's so not fair!" I said.

"Fair? Really?" Aiby said. "Is it fair that I have to put up with all your lies and excuses, like I'm one of the other people you make fun of?"

Warning! the voice in my head whispered.

I took a step back. I just couldn't understand why the conversation was going this way. I knew that girls were more complicated than boys, but this was even more confusing than normal. Instead of helping me out, she wanted to lecture me on lying, or something.

"Look, just give it a try," added Aiby. "Read the Scarsellis' instructions."

"Who are the Scarsellis?" I asked.

Aiby took the label out of my hand and waved it in my face. "The Scarsellis are one of the seven families of shopkeepers who take turns running the Enchanted Emporium. It's one of the very first things I taught you!"

"Oh, right, of course — the Scarsellis!" I said, trying

to remember the names of the other families. "And the Tiagos, or maybe Tios, the Van de Mayas . . . Oh, and the Askells — the worst of all of them. See, I remember!"

Aiby handed the label back to me with a smirk. "Good luck, Mr. Smarty-pants."

I pulled helplessly at the hand inside my pocket. "Please, Aiby," I begged. "Help me."

She made a zipping motion in front of her mouth. "You'll have to beg someone else, or do it yourself."

I nodded. "Okay then, I'll just go ask —"

"My dad wouldn't help you," she said. "Besides . . . he can't read the language anymore, anyway."

"Then why should I?!" I spat back.

"Because you're only thirteen!"

"I'm almost fourteen."

"And he's almost forty," Aiby said. She took a deep breath and let it out slowly. "See, you start to forget the Enchanted Language when you get older . . ."

"If I'm just going to eventually forget it," I said, "then why should I even bother to learn it?"

"Whatever," Aiby said. "I'm getting a snack."

Aiby went to a cupboard and pulled out a big jar of chocolate. With a knife, she spread it across two slices of bread. Then she left the Emporium while munching.

I called Patches, then started walking down the path next to the cliffs. When I turned to look back, Aiby had a big chocolate mustache on her face. Patches started to lick my ankle.

"Please, Aiby," I said.

"By the way, Finley," she said. Her smile made me nervous. "Don't you think I look tan?"

Red alert, red alert! a voice in my head said. *Don't answer that question, Finley.*

"And how did you get a tan?" I asked, immediately regretting it.

Aiby's smile was triumphant. "I went on a trip."

"A trip?" I asked.

"That's right. And I went with someone who knows languages much better than you do."

"Meb?"

"Try again."

I shrugged.

"I'll give you a hint," she said. "He's a boy, and he's really strong. And he actually listens to me once in a while. Unlike you."

I gaped at her. For the life of me, I couldn't understand why she was provoking me like this. "No," I said suddenly. "I don't believe it."

"You should," she said, and bit a big chunk of her bread. "Bye, Finley! And have a nice ride back home!"

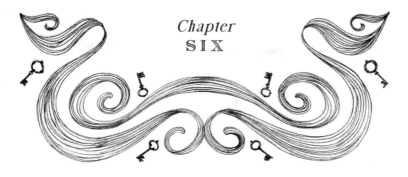

Chapter
SIX

JEALOUSY,
SHOCK,
& AWE

I biked home as fast as I could with one free hand, left Patches some water in a bowl in the kitchen, and then raced upstairs.

"DOUG!" I yelled in front of his bedroom door and opened it without waiting for a reply. My brother jumped out of his chair and hit the edge of his desk with his knees, sending a bunch of papers flying.

"Finley!" he howled, massaging his knees. "Are you crazy? You almost gave me a heart attack . . ."

Something isn't right, I thought. *When did Doug get a desk? And what were those pieces of paper that went flying? And that big book . . .*

"So it's true," I said through clenched teeth.

On the walls, where his favorite movie posters used to be, there was a big piece of paper. The sheet had a long list of letters written in the Enchanted Language and was stuck to the wall with tape.

I walked toward the piece of paper and touched it with my free hand.

"How did you . . . ?" I muttered.

As I ran my fingers over the strange letters, I couldn't decide if I felt shocked, jealous, betrayed, angry, or all of the above.

"Who taught you those words?" I finally asked.

"Which ones?" he asked.

"What does that word mean?" I said, pointing to a group of shimmering letters.

"It means that you should stop asking all these questions or I'm going to smack you," Doug said.

"Stop joking, Doug. I mean it."

Doug pointed at the sheet. "It's my name, doofus. And yours is beneath it."

Oh, right, I realized. Those were ten lines of "Doug" and "Finley" in the Enchanted Language. And then ten lines for "Aiby." Now I knew what that big book on Doug's desk was.

"You stole Aiby's vocabulary from me," I said. "You thief!"

"Relax," Doug said. "I didn't steal anything from anyone."

"It was in my room!"

My brother smirked. "Actually, it was underneath the bed in your room," he said. "And I didn't steal it, I just borrowed it. Permanently. Without asking you."

That was wittier than I thought Doug was capable of being. "You jerk — how would you like it if I snuck into your room and looked underneath your bed?"

"Be my guest," he said. "And while you're at it, you should tidy things up a bit."

I got right up in his face. "It was mine, Doug! MINE!"

Doug stood slowly. With him towering over me, my courage vanished pretty quickly. "So?" he said.

I tried to think, but all I could imagine was his fists smashing into my stomach.

"What's the matter with you?" Doug asked. He glanced down at my waist. "And why do you have your hand in that pocket?"

"Never mind," I said.

"Hey, listen up," he said. "If you don't get to the point here real fast, I'm going to throw you out the window. Got it?"

I decided not to call his bluff. "I just want to know why you chose to learn that stuff in my book," I said.

"Why do you think, Einstein?" he said, pointing at the top part of the paper on the wall.

I looked up to see Aiby's name written in the Enchanted Language.

"Did you guys go on a date?" I asked quietly.

Doug scratched his chin and grinned. "I see good news travels fast. Who told you?"

"Doesn't matter," I said, not wanting to believe it. Suddenly, someone — or something — pulled my hand hard from inside my pocket.

"It was amazing, bro," Doug said. "Really amazing. I ran into her less than a week ago . . ."

I gulped. *A week ago?* I thought. *What was I doing a week ago?*

"On Friday," Doug added.

What was I doing on Friday? I thought. I racked my brain but I couldn't remember.

"I met her outside the Greenlock Pub and bought a basket of fresh mussels," he said, talking like he was reading a romance novel. "I came up with the idea to tell her a few of the words that I'd taught myself from that book of yours . . ."

"It's called the Enchanted Language," I said, trying to sound like I knew what I was talking about.

"Well obviously," Doug said. "And I was all like —"

Doug slapped his hands together. "Man, you should have seen her face!"

I felt sick. My brother was clearly enjoying this. "What do you mean?" I asked in a scratchy voice. For some reason my mouth felt dry.

He tackled me onto his bed with a rugby move and ruffled my hair with his hands, like he always did whenever he was happy. "My little brother is so very curious!"

I tried to get free, but even with both hands it would've been unlikely. "Doug! I want to know what happened between you and Aiby!"

I blushed. He immediately stopped laughing and let me up. Then he placed his hands on his thighs and calmly asked, "Wow, Finley. Don't tell me you like that girl too!"

"No, I don't like her!" I yelled far too loudly to sound convincing. I calmed myself and did what I do best: make stuff up. "I do some work for them, is all. Aiby always says I don't make enough of an effort or understand what she means. You know how girls are, bro. I just never know what to say, so I was hoping to get some inside tips. You know, just between us guys."

To my complete shock, Doug bought it. "Oh. Okay. Now I get it. I almost had a heart attack. For a second

there, I thought we were fighting over a woman. Wouldn't that have been weird?! This morning, for instance, when we were on the boat . . ."

"YOU WERE ON A BOAT TOGETHER?!" I yelled, grabbing him by his shirt with my free hand.

"Dude, get your hand off me," he said quietly and pushed me up against the wall. "And don't yell. If dad finds out about this, I'm dead meat."

"What's with the boat ride, Doug?" I asked him quietly.

"It was Dogberry's boat," Doug said. "Since the old man died, no one uses it anymore."

Mr. Dogberry had died of a heart attack three weeks earlier. His farm was on the inland, not too far away from the ruins of the old, broken-down mansion that once belonged to the Lilys (which no longer existed on account of a stone giant walking over it).

"It looked so pathetic just sitting there all alone with no one to use it, so . . ."

"I don't care about the boat, Doug," I said. "I want to know about Aiby."

"She didn't care who owned that boat," Doug said with a grin. "Actually, she told me it was a really nice boat."

I sighed and rolled my eyes. Not for the first time, I wondered if Doug was messing with me.

"So we paddled toward Callakille and Robha Chuaig. When we got closer to Reginald Bay, Aiby asked me to stop. She sat there and looked at her house for a while. Then we crossed the bay until Rona island, and . . . well, let's just say I was lucky I had gas for the motor when we got there because it was an exhausting ride."

I'd been asking dad to take me to the islands for years. To So Rona, Raasay, Scalpay, and Skyle. Or at least Crowlin and Sgeir Thraid and the Sgeir Dhearg twin cliffs. I would've settled for Guillaman — I just wanted to try to send a few messages in bottles so I could figure out how the ones I'd found had gotten to Applecross.

"And then what?" I asked.

Doug shrugged. "We got to the island trail. No one was there except for us. She was looking out at the sea, sniffing the air, and looking for some rocks to bring back home. That's when I . . ." He trailed off.

My eyes went wide. "You what, Doug." It wasn't much of a question. I knew what was coming.

"I kissed her," he said.

I felt like I'd become a tree, my roots planted deep beneath the floor. I thought of all the cusses and curses

that Sammy Monkfish had written in his dirty notepad, but none of them accurately captured the spirit of what I wanted to say.

"Actually," Doug said. "I didn't really kiss her. Let's just say I hugged her and I tried to kiss her, and wow . . . you should have been there. It was like trying to smooch a frozen porcupine."

I squinted. "Really?" I asked.

He shot me a weird look. "Yep. I got stone cold rejected."

I breathed a quiet but deep sigh of relief. Neither of us said anything for a solid minute.

Maybe Doug can read that label Aiby gave me, I realized. I handed him the label. "Can you read what this says?"

He held the label comically close to his face and read slowly. "Do not wash for any reason. Insert one object into pocket at a time. Above all else, do not hold the hand." Doug looked up at me. "What the crap is this?"

"That's all it says?" I asked. "Nothing else?"

Doug continued reading. "In case of problems, place the label inside the pocket." Doug handed the label back to me. "So what does it mean?"

"Oh, nothing," I lied. "I just wanted to see if you had really learned how to read the language."

I quickly put the label inside my pocket. Just like that, the hand in my bottomless pants pocket released its grip. I sighed, massaging my freed fingers.

Doug shrugged and walked toward the door. "You know what?" he said, turning back to face me.

"What?"

"We're the same age."

"Who?"

"Aiby and I. She said she's sixteen, just like me."

"Great," I mumbled.

"What?"

"Nothing. Nothing."

If Aiby was really sixteen, it meant I was at least two years younger than her.

"More bad news," I mumbled.

The Enchanted Language

The Enchanted language belonged to Ben Laquedem's collection
in Turin, Italy, before it passed to King Vittorio Amedeo the
Second's library. It's missing pages 197, 313, and 616, and
bears a dedication to a mysterious lady named Beatrice.

BEACHES,
DISTRACTIONS,
& WORK

The following morning, my dad drove me to Reverend Prospero's place. I obeyed my mother's command and wore my only suit.

"I look like a penguin," I said.

"No, you look like a young man," Dad said, which probably really meant, "I pity you."

Dad's mood hadn't improved from the previous evening. In fact, it had gotten worse. All the way from the farm to the village, my dad chewed his nails and said next to nothing.

After he dropped me off at the reverend's house, Dad said he was headed to the village pub where he was supposed to meet up with another farmer. I asked if he

was having problems with his sheep, but he just left me in a cloud of exhaust.

"Let's go talk to Mr. Everett," the reverend said. He grabbed a horrible black hat off his coat hanger and slapped it on his head. I'd seen him wearing it a lot lately to protect himself from the heat, which was hilarious for two reasons. First, it looked really tiny on his gigantic noggin. Second, Applecross hardly got any sun with all the clouds in the sky.

I followed the reverend as he walked. "I don't understand what my new job is, Reverend," I said. "All my dad told me was that I'd be a 'beach tester.'"

The reverend kept walking quickly along the road. "Neither do, I actually," he said. "But it could be fun, don't you think? I mean, you'll be on the beach!"

"Are you sure?" I asked.

"No," the reverend admitted. "But if Mr. Everett really needs a young man to test the beaches in Applecross, and he can pay for it, I don't see why it shouldn't be you. If nothing else, it'll add to your résumé."

I had my doubts, but I kept them to myself.

It turned out that the job was for real. Mr. Everett was an eccentric, retired professor who had opened a small tourist shop in Applecross for some reason. The Curious Traveler's front window overlooked the main square, if you could even call it a square, and he almost always sat in a wicker chair right by the shop's door. He had recently added a desk so he could play cards with himself.

As soon as he saw us coming, he gathered up his cards and slipped them into his pocket. "Hello, Reverend," he said, and gave me a funny look.

I bent over to pick up a card that had fallen on the ground. I noticed that underneath the desk there were some multicolored bugs — just like the ones that had crawled out from Adele Babele's hair.

Weird, I thought.

The strange card was a grimy, yellow jack. But the weirdest thing about it was that the jack's face looked just like a dog's.

I gave it back to Professor Everett. He thanked me and quickly pocketed it. "The editors of a tourist book called *The All Together World* called me a while back. You two know about them, right?"

I shrugged. I had never been a tourist. In fact, the farthest I'd gone was across the country to watch my brother's team lose at rugby.

"They're making a new edition for Scotland," he said, glancing through his glasses at some notes. "The most requested topics of interest were beaches and waves,

because of the surfers. They're looking for unique places to surf, which they refer to as hot spots. In short, they need someone to spend a day on each beach in the area to document the waves and beach conditions."

"Are they also willing to pay something for Finley's time?" asked the reverend.

"Of course," Mr. Everett said.

The reverend gave me a hard pat on the back. "What do you say, Finley?" he asked. "Granted, you aren't really dressed for the job."

I sighed with relief and immediately loosened my tie. "Anything's fine with me if I don't have to wear this dumb suit," I said. "When do I begin?"

Mr. Everett smiled. "We'll get you started shortly," he said. "Just give me some time to call the guys from the guide to update them. Do you have a method of transportation, Finley? A boat, or maybe a motorbike?"

Reverend Prospero laughed. "Perhaps he has a car, Mr. Everett? And a beard? He's just a kid!"

I rolled my eyes. "I have a bicycle," I said.

"That'll do," said Reverend Prospero. He explained to Mr. Everett that my salary should be paid to the church. Then he tipped his funny little hat and headed back down the road.

Mr. Everett looked me up and down. "You should

probably wear some clothes that are more comfortable next time," he said.

I rolled my eyes. "Thanks, Mom," I said. "The suit was a great idea."

Mr. Everett frowned, then produced some keys from his pocket. He handed me one. "This is for my new tenant in the apartment at the back of my shop," he said. He handed me another key. "Use this if the door's locked. Leave your things back there, and take a notebook with you. Is there anything else you need?"

"Oh, yes," I answered, pocketing the keys. "Can I take Patches to work with me?"

* * *

And that was how I became the first beach tester in Applecross history. Believe it or not, the job was actually kind of challenging. First, I had to highlight the position of every beach on a map of Applecross. Second, I had to use a towel to measure the beach's space to see how many people could be tanning there at the same time. Third, I had to use a tape measure to determine how far into the sea the water remained shallow. Fourth, I used a graduated scale to measure the average height of the waves. Finally, there was a questionnaire to fill out about the sand or rocks, nearby cliffs, seaweed deposits, and any nearby landmarks like the arched rock of Ard na Claise Moire. I was required to stay on each beach for three hours. After all that, I had to give each beach a rating of one to five stars based on everything I'd observed.

As I worked, I obsessively imagined the conversation between Aiby and my brother, word for word. When I wasn't doing that, various other questions filled my mind.

Why was the world so unfair?

What was I doing with my life?

What is the meaning of my existence?

Why wasn't I born a dog, like Patches, so I could be happy just chasing seagulls like he was doing right now?

I sighed. I wasn't depressed, I was just in shock or something. But there wasn't anything I could do about that, so I decided to focus on my new job the best I could.

I rode my bike back and forth along the coastal road, stopping every time I found a beach where I could lay my towel down for measurements. After that, I used the measuring tape and the weird tool that measured the waves to collect data, then wrote it in my notebook. As long as I kept myself busy, my mind stayed off Aiby and my brother at least.

I did occasionally start to wonder about Professor Everett. Even before the Enchanted Emporium had opened, I suspected he knew more about magical things than what little he claimed. I once found a strange list of names inside his store that included the Lilys and the Askells. Mr. Everett also seemed like the kind of person who said one thing while thinking about three others.

Eventually, Doug and Aiby crept back into my thoughts, so I tried to think about my dad's sheep and why he'd seemed so worried that morning.

I thought about sheep for the rest of the day. It was really annoying, but much better than the alternative.

Chapter
EIGHT

A BAD DRIVER,
A STRANGE MEETING,
& MCBLACK

The second day of work, I almost got run over by Jules's terrible red van. He was a maniac on the roads, what with his windows down and ABBA blaring from his stereo. The first time he drove by me, he waved and smirked at me while forcing me off the road. I ended up in a ditch with my bike on top of me.

I was livid. Immediately, I jumped back on my bike and pedaled toward town to complain to Reverend Prospero. That man and his van needed to be stopped, no matter the cost.

As it turned out, I wasn't the only one who wanted the reverend's help. There were a few people standing outside Maelrubha church, and my dad was among them.

I climbed off my bike. "Shh, Patches," I whispered. "Let's sneak closer to hear what they're saying."

My dad and the others were in the middle of a heated conversation. Some of the participants seemed upset. Others just shook their heads in the typical Scottish manner and impatiently waited for their turn to speak.

"Three of my sheep disappeared in one week!" one farmer said. "And I saw a fourth trying to jump the fence today."

"Yes!" another farmer said. "Mine are acting strange too!"

"And someone cut my shrimp net," one of the fishermen said. "The entire thing was torn apart. I've never seen such a thing before."

"Well I heard my sheep bleating at the moon!" a third man said. I thought the idea of a were-sheep was hilarious, but no one seemed to be laughing.

Another man held out a piece of rotten wood for the group to see. "This is a piece of my fence. It looks like some *thing* took a big bite out of it!"

Another man stepped forward to look at it closer. "Interesting. I found some bones close to the woods, and let me tell you . . . they're from an animal. A *big* one."

A few farmers gasped. One of them made the sign of the cross, which I thought was a little overdramatic.

"Something destroyed my shrubs as well!" a woman cried. "It looks like they've been burnt, but no one saw a fire."

"It's thieves! It must be thieves!" a man shouted.

"But why would anyone bother us?" another said. "I mean, why would anybody poke two holes in my boats? It just doesn't make sense."

I saw heads shaking, hands gesturing wildly, and arms crossed in suspicion. The most amazing thing about the scene was that fishermen and shepherds were united in something for once. Typically, they would only see eye to eye if there was a conflict with someone from somewhere outside Applecross, like Lochalsh or Skyle. I've known from an early age that the Scottish love nothing more than to draw lines in the dirt and pick sides. So while it was possible the problems were just silly superstitions and coincidences, the fact that all these people were united in concern made that seem unlikely.

"It all started when they opened the camping area," said a man with a sour face.

"That's nonsense, Barragh!" my dad said. "What does that have to do with my missing sheep?"

"If it's not an animal's doing, then someone stole them!" Barragh said. "And I strongly doubt it was one of us."

"Gentlemen!" boomed the reverend. "Please — no arguing."

"And what about the death of old lady Cumai?" Barragh asked.

"She was over eighty, the poor woman. Isn't that explanation enough for her passing?" dad said.

"But she was so healthy!" Barragh argued.

I realized I'd seen him before, but couldn't remember where. "Last month it was Dogberry, and now old lady Cumai!" Barragh added.

"You're being ridiculous, Barragh!" my dad said. "Of the thousand inhabitants of Applecross, more than half are older than seventy. Death is an unfortunate but common result for them. There's no reason to think foul play was involved in Cumai's passing."

"What about the fact that the mill always has its lights on?" Barragh challenged. "A lot of people have seen the lights from the village, but if you go to check, there's no one there!" His face was flushed.

"Gentlemen, please!" the reverend said. "Let the dead rest in peace, and let us concentrate on the missing sheep."

"And the fish," one of the fishermen said.

"I say we need a detective," another said.

"Maybe a vet would be better — a real vet, not just a

farmer," one man said. Then he glanced at my dad. "No offence, McPhee."

My dad rolled his eyes. "Why do we need a vet? To tell us that our sheep are missing?"

"A vet won't be any help figuring out who destroyed my nets," a fisherman said. "We need a detective."

"What if we organized some sort of night watch?"

"That would cost less than hiring a cop or detective."

Everyone agreed with that. We Scottish love the idea of saving money.

"We could have groups of two or three villagers, with rifles, patrol the fences of the farms were the sheep disappeared."

"Yes! That way we'll catch them — sooner or later."

The men talked for a few more minutes, eventually deciding to meet up that evening at the pub to sort out the details. Then most of the villagers departed, leaving my dad, Barragh, and the reverend. I joined them, pretending to have just arrived.

When my dad saw me approach, he pointed in my direction. "We could ask the Lilys for help," he said. "My son says they're intelligent people who have traveled all over the world. Perhaps an outside opinion would be useful to us . . ."

Reverend Prospero nodded in agreement, but

Barragh grunted. "Do you know what I think, Camas?" he asked.

Barragh had used my father's first name. Whenever I heard it spoken, I swelled with pride, for Camas McPhee was a great name — just trust me on that one.

"I'm no psychic, McBlack," my father said through clenched teeth.

That's why he looks familiar! I realized. The McBlacks were the crankiest family in the county. They lived in a lonely little house nicknamed Scary Villa on an island across the bay. Nearly no one in Applecross went there, and the McBlacks almost never came down to the village.

"I don't trust the Lilys at all," Barragh McBlack said. "Not one bit."

My dad snorted. "That doesn't surprise me. Does your family trust anybody?"

"I'm not joking around here," Barragh said. "We can't underestimate the danger we're facing."

"Don't be ridiculous," my dad said. "This is nothing supernatural or strange. We'll figure it out if we work together."

For a few long moments, no one said anything.

"She registered for the marathon, you know," Reverend Prospero said, breaking the silence.

My dad raised an eyebrow and Barragh tilted his head. "Who?" my dad asked.

"Old lady Cumai," the reverend said. "She was very sporty, you know. You see, she was training for the Loch Ness marathon in September."

"So she was fit? Then it's even more suspicious that she died of a heart attack," McBlack said. "Something strange is going on . . ."

For the first time that night, I agreed with Barragh McBlack: it was pretty weird for an eighty-year-old woman to be training for a marathon.

Chapter
NINE

A MAN,
A BOY,
& A FATHER

Later that evening, Dad ate dinner by himself, then told my mom he was leaving again to go check on the Mulligans' place with the rest of the night watch. My mom asked him if he was sure that was a good idea, but he left without answering her.

Outside, I heard the truck's engine struggle to turn over before it started. As Dad pulled away, Doug told me that our sheep had been acting really weird lately. Instead of grazing out in the fields, they huddled together near the farm — far away from the woods.

Dad stayed out past midnight. When he finally got home, even from my bedroom I could tell he was exhausted. I heard him shuffle his feet, throw his

boots on the floor, and stomp up the stairs like his legs were cinder blocks. Whatever he and the other watch members had been looking for, they hadn't found it.

Meanwhile, I couldn't sleep. I admit, I was scared. Scared of whatever it was that broke the nets in the bay and stole the sheep. I could tell Patches was nervous, too, by the way he flailed his paws in the air while he slept like he was trying to run away from a nightmare.

I sighed. "There's no way I'm getting any sleep tonight."

I jumped out of bed and glanced out the window. There were countless shining stars in the sky. For some reason, their cold and distant twinkling made me feel like my problems weren't a really big deal.

Aiby and Doug, sheep thieves, tattered fishnets . . . none of it was really worth worrying about, though old lady Cumai's death was a real bummer. After all, she would've been the perfect person to help me solve all the odd mysteries that were happening in town. She seemed to know everything — lots of weird stories about things like magical creatures of the sea. For a while now, I'd been meaning to visit her and ask her to tell me some of them again. But I kept postponing the trip, and now it was too late.

I glanced out at the pasture. I saw a man. He was standing in the field near the edge of the woods.

And he was staring right at my house.

I was paralyzed. I couldn't look away. The man was draped in shadow, but something sparkled in his face. It reminded me of the light in the rearview mirror of my dad's van whenever he drove away from me.

He was a big guy and wore a long cape that looked like it was made from many different pieces of fabric. His hands were in front of his chest, and he kept repeating this weird gesture, almost as if he was praying, then stopping, then praying again.

I narrowed my eyes. There was no doubt about it: he was looking right at me.

"Patches!" I whispered in the dark.

My friend leaped to my side. Together, we snuck downstairs without making a peep. When I pushed the screen door open, I felt shivers run down my spine and through my bare feet.

I slowly left the house. Patches sniffed the air.

The man was gone.

"He was just there," I said, pointing at the end of the grass and the fence. "Right over there by the edge of the woods."

Without thinking, I began sprinting across the grass toward the woods. As I ran barefoot in the moonlight in pursuit of the shadow of a man I saw from the window of my house, I began to worry that I'd lost my mind. At the same time, I had this weird sensation that I was exactly where I was supposed be. As if all this madness made perfect sense in some way.

One thing was for sure: I certainly felt alive.

So who was that man? And why was he there? I thought as my feet slapped against the grass. *And what was he doing with his hands?*

Patches let out little barks as he followed at my heels. His presence gave me comfort. When we reached the point where I'd seen that weird man, Patches nudged his nose into the ground and sniffed.

"Can you smell him, Patches? Can you?"

Patches growled. His fur stood up on his neck.

"Good boy," I told him, relieved to know I hadn't lost my mind. "Where did he go, huh? Did he run into the woods, boy?"

I placed my hands on the fence and traced an imaginary path with my eyes that the man might have taken. *Who could he be?* I wondered. *A cattle thief, a hunter? A homeless person?*

A voice in my head kept telling me to go back inside, but I jumped over the fence and Patches scurried under it. Together, we walked toward the woods.

The stars above looked particularly bright that night. As we neared the forest, I saw that some leaves on the closest trees were shaking despite the lack of a breeze. I wondered if the man had brushed against them as he'd made his escape.

The grass was dried out and dead where the man had been standing. Burnt. I kneeled to take a closer look, and Patches nuzzled up next to me. I found myself running my hand through his warm fur.

Go back inside, a little voice in my head said. Just then, I heard a voice come from the woods. It sounded sweet like honey. I felt strangely compelled to enter the woods.

As I stepped into the tree line, I heard the sound of grass and branches being crunched underfoot. I tensed my muscles and prepared for the worst.

"Finley?" someone called out for me.

I turned to see my dad standing on the other side of the fence. His feet were bare, his hair was a mess, and he didn't have a shirt on. He held his old rifle in his hands, the barrel sparkling menacingly in the moonlight. "Is that you, Finley?"

I gulped. Slowly, I walked toward the fence and raised my hand to make sure he knew who I was.

"Get back to the house! Now!" my dad yelled.

I glanced at the woods, then down at the footprints in the dead grass. The strange noise I'd heard coming from the woods was gone now. Once again, I wondered if I'd imagined everything.

I jumped back over the fence and followed my dad to the house. Patches followed me. Both of us glanced back at the woods every few steps.

"What were you doing over there?" my dad asked. He wasn't looking at me. Instead, his eyes were focused on his sheep huddling nearby.

"I don't know," I said. I pointed at the place where I saw the man. "I thought I saw someone standing by the edge of the woods."

Dad slowly lowered his rifle. "You were probably dreaming," he suggested.

"No, Dad, I swear! I saw a man — a really tall guy wearing a long cape. But he didn't look very dangerous to me."

"We'll talk about it tomorrow," he said. "Come on inside, we'll keep watch for the rest of the night from the kitchen."

As we entered the house, we closed the windows and our old front door. Dad made some coffee while I leaned against the counter. We stared out the window, neither of us saying a single word.

Then, when the morning light crept over the horizon, we finally went to bed.

Chapter
TEN

A WEIRD MAN,
MORE MYSTERIES,
& MAGIC COOKIES

I felt really weird the next day, and it wasn't because I was exhausted from the lack of sleep. Every single noise and every little breeze gave me goose bumps. Every sudden movement made me shiver.

"Is everything okay, Fin?" my mom asked, noticing I wasn't eating my breakfast.

"Yes." Her voice was irritating to me, like the sound of white noise.

Dad was already gone when I'd woken up. I asked Mom where he went.

"He took the van somewhere," she said. "To town, I think."

I grabbed my mug of coffee and left the kitchen. As I stepped outside, the daylight made the field look much smaller than the previous night. That was confusing because it felt like I'd run for quite some time in the dark.

I walked toward the fence. Patches followed by my side. When we reached it, he jumped backward and barked at the woods. The grass seemed normal now. There weren't any dark or burnt spots visible.

I shrugged and headed back toward the farm. I spotted my brother moving some bags of animal feed. "Hey, Doug," I said.

"What's up?" he said without stopping.

"Have you ever heard anything about men living in the woods?"

He looked at me in surprise. "What do you mean?"

"Men living in the woods," I repeated. "Ever heard of anything like that?"

"Why would men live in the woods?" he asked.

"I don't know," I said. "That's why I was asking."

Doug shrugged and kept working, so I left before he could ask me to help him.

I brought the mug back inside the house, devoured a slice of warm pie that my mom had just baked, and hopped on my bike. I had the beach testing notebook with me, but I didn't feel like working. I had too much

on my mind. Instead, I biked the coastal road along the river, the mill, and the cliffs, heading toward Reginald Bay. Toward the Enchanted Emporium.

I jumped off my bike as soon as I got to the weird sign with the arrow. Together, Patches and I crossed through the woods to the road on the small bay. Patches immediately began to chase the many seagulls in the area.

Moments later, we were in front of a familiar red building. The Enchanted Emporium's front door was open.

"Aiby!" I called. "Are you home?"

A seagull flew over my head, let out a cry, then disappeared over the sea.

I waited. "Aiby?"

I felt like I'd gone back in time to when I'd first stood in front of that door with my mailbag and a strange letter in my hands.

Finally, Aiby leaned out the window on the second floor. She wore her usual, brilliant smile that I liked so much. You know, the kind of smile that means someone is happy to see you.

"So you saved yourself from your pants!" she said.

"You mean your dad's pants," I said.

She leaned further out the window and smiled

sweetly. In that moment, I heard every sound in the entire bay: the waves, the seagulls, and most of all, my rapid heartbeat.

"Are you coming down?" I asked.

"Do you have mail for me?"

"No. But we have to talk."

"Someone strange is in Applecross," I said as soon as she appeared in the doorway.

She had a cup of milk and a box with her. The label read:

Dark Chocolate

Grimm Cookies

"Just one strange person?" she said, gesturing for me to follow her. We stopped at the edge of the cliffs. I saw that the steps on the staircase leading down to the water had been repaired.

"My dad wants to build a small dock for himself," Aiby said. "It'd be nice to have a boat, don't you think?"

"Sure," I said, but all I could think about was Doug's boating adventure with her.

"He went to town to buy some wood for the steps," she said.

We sat down and glanced out at the sea far below us. "So, who's this strange someone?" Aiby asked.

"Actually, I don't really know," I said. "I saw him last night — well, actually this morning, from my bedroom window about an hour or two before sunrise. He was across the field, near the woods. And . . . he was staring at me."

Aiby opened the box. I saw there were two cookies inside. She grabbed one. I tried to grab the last one but she stopped me. "Wait," she said, and closed the box. She dunked her cookie in the cup of milk and then ate it. "Welcome to the cookie challenge! See, you have to dunk the cookie in the milk as far as you can without the cookie breaking," she said while chewing. "If the cookie breaks and falls in, you lose."

When she opened the box again, there were two cookies inside. "Whoa!" I said. "Are these . . . magic cookies?"

"The box is getting old, I think," she said. "Not that long ago, it became filled with cookies every time you closed it, but I think it got damaged when we moved. You have to remember to leave at least one in the box before closing it, or it won't refill."

I frowned at her. "Aiby, did you hear what I told you?"

"Did you hear what I told *you*?" she asked.

I grabbed a cookie and put it inside the milk. "Yes," I said. "But what I'm talking about is serious."

"Everything is serious," she said.

I dunked the cookie about halfway into her milk. Immediately, it split in two and the bottom half fell into the milk.

"Like I said, everything is serious," she said. "But it's difficult to determine the right moment to discuss something in particular."

I grunted, stood, and walked a few steps away from her. Sitting there in the sun, Aiby's skin gleamed like bronze, and her dark freckles made her eyes look even greener than normal.

"You're going to make me ask, aren't you?" I said.

Aiby closed and reopened the box. "Ask me what?"

"You know what I mean."

"I do?" she asked. Her cookie crumbled onto her weird, multicolored t-shirt. Whenever she wore it, she reminded me of an ancient princess.

I sighed, realizing I'd have to say the words. "When are you going to tell me the truth about . . . you and Doug?"

Aiby's eyes opened wide. "Huh? Me and Doug?"

"The truth, Aiby. I can handle it."

Aiby laughed her musical laugh. "I have no idea what you're talking about."

It seemed like she was making fun of me, so I started to walk away.

"Finley?" she called after me, but I didn't stop.

"I get it," I said over my shoulder. "I mean, there's nothing wrong with going on a boat trip with Doug, but why do it without telling me? There's nothing more selfish than —"

"Boredom," Aiby said.

I stopped. A nearby seagull was staring at me like it was interested in whether I was going to stay or leave. "What did you say?" I asked without turning around.

"I said that I went with Doug to look for the Flowers of Boredom. You know, for Adele Babele's order."

I blinked a few times, unsure what to say next. "And how does one find Flowers of Boredom?" I asked.

Aiby chuckled. "How do you think, Mr. Smarty-pants?" Aiby teased. I heard the box close and then reopen.

"You know," I said. "Eating all those cookies can't be good for you."

"Are you worried about me, Finley?" she said.

More teasing, I thought.

I sighed and started walking away. Just then, the seagull flew into the sky. A moment later, Aiby's hand

spun me around to face her. I found myself embraced in a hug. The tip of my nose rested on her neck, and her long hair brushed against my face.

"Finley," she said, holding me tight. "Now that I've had my breakfast, how about you tell me why you really came here?"

I couldn't remember why I'd come to see her, but I didn't really care. In that moment, all I wanted was to stay right there in her arms forever.

Gently, she pulled away from me. "Well?" she said, smiling warmly.

I felt warm and woozy, but I managed to say, "A strange man came from the woods and stared at my house last night," I said quietly. "I've never seen him before."

"A strange man?" she asked.

"He looked . . . different than normal men," I said.

"Different . . . as in magical?" she asked.

I nodded. Sometimes it felt like she could read my mind. "Yes, that's right," I said. "Magical . . . and dangerous."

Chapter
ELEVEN

LATIN,
INSTRUMENTS,
& DREAMS

To figure out who (or what) I'd seen in the field the previous night, Aiby brought me to her family's library. Whenever Aiby needed information, she paged through her family's extensive library in search of answers. The Lily family had specialized in books ever since their ancestors first opened their version of the Enchanted Emporium.

Just like the Lilys, each family of magical shopkeepers had different specialties. The Scarsellis, for example, specialized in clothing, accessories, and jewelry. The Tiago family focused on hot air balloons, magic tricks, and tools for divination, or reading the future. The Askells trafficked in the afterlife, and were known to do so in dangerous ways.

103

The Lily family's library had books filled with magic spells and recipes (spells worked outside the body while recipes worked internally). They had maps of this world, and many others, along with countless tomes on other subjects. My favorite was the *Book of Reading in the Dark*, which could only be read when held in front of a mirror.

Aiby was standing on a wheeled ladder. She began to browse the highest shelves, under the section dedicated to the subject of "men."

Aiby read the titles aloud. *"Extraordinary Men, Blue Men, Men of Silence . . ."*

It was impossible to tell how many different magical books were in that library. "How in the world did you and your father get all these books here?" I asked.

"We freeze-dried them with an old recipe from the Cathars," she said. "Then we returned them to normal size with a special ink."

"You're kidding," I said.

Aiby just smiled and kept searching. While she browsed the books, I examined a gorgeous porcelain pot that contained a single bonsai tree. I gently touched one of the fruits on its branches, and I heard a solemn voice: "Moldrige Lily, born in Leipzig on May 5, 1754. Died in Tangier on July 12, 1808." Then it kept repeating itself, over and over.

"Ah!" I cried, taking a quick step back. "How do I turn this thing off?"

"Slap your hand on the pot," Aiby said indifferently.

I did it, and the tree stopped repeating itself. "What was that?"

Aiby looked at me. "It's our family tree," she said, like it was the most normal thing in the world. Then she titled her head and added, "Ah! Good thing I looked at you — the book we need is right next to you!"

She climbed down quickly and grabbed a large book off a desk that was next to me. "Woodsmen!" she said proudly.

The book's title, printed in red letters on the wooden cover, read:

The Black Book of the Woods:
Anomalies, Fires, and Fearsome Creatures

"Dang," I muttered, turning the book over in my hands. "It would take me three months to read this whole thing . . ."

"Three months, or a Critical Strainer," she whispered. "We should have one somewhere around here. Come with me!"

"Sprunfz!" the Gardener of Pages greeted us in the laboratory. Aiby produced a big rectangular strainer

from under a table, then grabbed a handful of white paper.

We went to Aiby's bedroom. She set the sheets of paper on the floor and held the book over them, face down. "Give me a hand?" she asked.

"Sure, but how?" I said.

"Hold the Critical Strainer," she said. "And repeat this magic formula . . ."

"You know I can't read the Enchanted Language, Aiby," I said.

"It is in Latin, Finley," Aiby said. "And you've spoken Latin before . . ."

Something clicked inside my head, as if a trapdoor had suddenly snapped open after being sealed shut for many years. I remembered what the words meant: *Power arises from brevity.*

Before I knew what was happening, the phrase sprang from my lips like it was my native tongue. Tiny black drops of ink began to fall from the Critical Strainer. As the drops hit the paper, they began to squirm around like gnats.

"More," Aiby urged me.

I shivered, but repeated the phrase and waved the strainer.

"Again," she said.

I shook the strainer faster and faster and the black ink drops began to rain down like sleet.

"That's enough, Finley," Aiby said. She bent down to pick up the papers, then showed them to me. They were completely covered with words! "Here is a summary of the parts of this book that might help us."

"How the heck did the strainer know what we were interested in?" I asked.

Aiby snorted. "It's a magical item, Finley. If you think too much about how it works, then it'll stop working."

I put down the Critical Strainer. "And how did you know that I'd already spoken Latin?" I asked.

Aiby hid her face behind her hair. Earlier, when she'd hugged me, she'd seemed older than me. She'd explained everything like she was my big sister. But now, she seemed smaller and frightened. And a little annoyed.

"Because . . . I talked to someone who taught you," she said in a low voice. "Maybe in our dreams."

I felt a long shiver run down my spine, and realized that some part of me understood even though I had no idea what Aiby was talking about. Someone from my dreams had taught me Latin, which was weird because I hardly ever remember my dreams. But I often remembered forgetting them, if that makes sense.

In any case, I knew I'd been dreaming for a very long time . . . I just didn't know what I'd been dreaming about.

"I think I understand," I said.

And once again, a voice inside my head whispered, *Get out of there, Finley. Before it's too late.*

Get out of there.

E. T. STARR.

The CRITICAL STRAINER

No. 30.843. Patented Dec. 4. 1860.

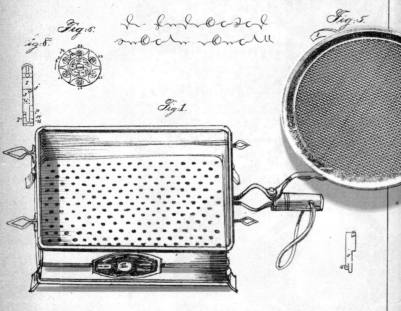

This highly practical magical object was in high demand during the 16th and 17th centuries when printed books boomed and no one had time to read them all. It sifts through the most interesting topics inside any book and summarizes them in two to three pages. Since a reader's interests often change, sifting a book multiple times will likely produce different results.

Witnesses

ENCHANTED EMPORIUM

Inventor

Chapter
TWELVE

BOOKS,
BROTHERS,
& GREEN MEN

We sat on the floor with the sheets of paper in our hands. Patches was glad we were working at his height, and thanked us with affectionate licks from time to time.

I read aloud. "'Men who live in the woods are called Green Men, or sylvan men. Green is considered to be the color of the fairies, and for this reason many Scots refuse to wear green for fear of annoying the Green Men. Green is also the color of life and of nature, which is neither good nor evil.'"

Aiby began to read. "'There is a poem called *Sir Gawain and the Green Knight* written by an unknown medieval author. In that story, Sir Gawain, nephew of King Arthur, is visited on New Year's Eve by a strange,

green man with a branch of holly in one hand and a large axe in the other.'"

"That's interesting, I guess," I said, "but that doesn't sound like the man from last night. I did see him do something with his hands, though. Something like this." I imitated his movements by rubbing my hands in front my chest.

Aiby shrugged, then continued reading. "'The Green Man challenges Sir Gawain to strike him with his axe, but on one condition: the following year, Gawain must allow the Green Man to return the favor.'"

I chuckled. "That's ridiculous. How could anyone possibly survive an axe wound?"

Aiby smiled. "'Sir Gawain accepts the challenge,'" she read, "'and lops off the Green Man's head with a single blow.'"

"See?" I said. "The Green Man wasn't too bright —"

Aiby holds up her finger to silence me and continues reading. "'To Gawain's surprise, the Green Man stands up, thanks him, picks up his own head, holds it under his arm, and makes an appointment for the following year to fulfill his end of the bargain. A year later, Sir Gawain goes to the meeting as promised, and the Green Man thanks him for having kept the agreement.'"

I raised an eyebrow. "Did the Green Man kill Gawain?" I asked.

Aiby scanned the text. "No," she said. "It seems all that he wanted was to find an honorable man who knew the importance of respecting agreements. To reward him, the Green Man gives Gawain great courage by revealing to him how to deal with any kind of fear. The text goes on to explain that the Green Man of the poem plays a dual role: challenge and reward, danger and safety, friend and enemy."

I shivered, then went back to reading the sheets. "'He can have many names,'" I read. "'He is sometimes called the Silvano, the Woodwose, or just the Outlaw. He is a wild and unpredictable creature, endowed with supernatural strength. Men of this nature have been spotted all over the world.'" I looked up at Aiby. "It doesn't mention anything about disappearing sheep or damaged farms."

"Keep reading," Aiby murmured.

"'Whoever has met a Green Man inevitably describes him as a powerful creature with a face made of fog, and long, wild hair encrusted with chunks of bark. They are said to smell like soil, have rough and hasty manners, and have long, bushy beards.'"

Aiby elbowed me in the arm. "Does that sound like your strange man?" she asked.

"Maybe," I whispered. "I saw that the grass seemed burned or singed where he'd been standing. I remember my dad saying that someone in the village found their bushes burnt as well. Do the papers mention anything like that?"

Aiby checked the pages. "No," she said. "On the contrary, it says the Green Man is considered to be a guardian of nature, often armed with a bow, arrows, and a long horn."

I shook my head. "That's not right, then," I said. "Maybe we're on the wrong track here."

"Did he wear a turban?" Aiby asked.

"What? No, why?"

"It says here that there's an Eastern version of the Green Man, called the Khidr, and that he was the assistant to Alexander the Great. It says he came into possession of a copy of the will of Adam, the supposed first man." Aiby looked at me with wide eyes. "And that the will contained directions to a miraculous fountain beyond Olaf Mountain in the center of a place named the Land of Darkness."

"Cheerful," I muttered, scratching my dog's ears.

"I guess the Khidr found it and drank from it," Aiby said. She read aloud again, "'The liquid was watery, but whiter than milk, cooler than ice, sweeter than honey, softer than butter, and more fragrant than the scent of musk. Khidr became immortal . . . and completely green. Since then, he occasionally appears in the dreams of magical or mystical people to show them the way.'"

Aiby was staring at me. "Don't look at me like that," I said. "I'm not a magical or mystical person, and when I saw him I was wide awake, not dreaming. Just ask Patches."

Aiby chuckled. "Right. I'll keep reading," she said. A moment later, she pointed at a specific part of a sheet. "It seems the Critical Strainer considered this story to be very important: it's about two so-called green children, written by Thomas Keightley."

"Who is he?" I asked.

"I've never heard of him before, but he writes about two siblings with green arms and legs who were found in the woods next to a cave." Aiby read aloud, "'The two children did not speak any known languages, nor did they eat meat. They were taken to the village of St. Mary, but the boy died a few days later. The female, however, lived a long time without ever growing old. Over the years, she learned to speak. She said that she came from a village where no one ever saw the sun, and that she had been in charge of the sheep — until their herds began to disappear.'"

"Here we go!" I exclaimed. "Keep reading."

"'One day, the girl and her brother saw some sheep enter a cave. As they neared the cave, they heard strange music coming from inside. The two children entered the cave and were soon lost in the dark, until they reached another entrance to the cave, where they were found . . .'" The text ran off the page. Aiby searched for the next sheet, but it was blank.

"Weird," Aiby said. "The story seems to just end there."

"No!" I said. "There has to be more — keep looking."

Aiby shuffled through the pages. "I don't see it here," she said.

I sighed and stood. As I glanced out the window over the fields of grass, the wind seemed to be calling my name. It urged me to cross the fence and enter the woods. I felt a thrill run down my spine, accompanied by fear. I wondered if that story had more to do with Applecross's recent events than I could ever imagine.

I rubbed my temples, thinking again about the

reflection of the light I'd seen in the face of the strange man. I looked down at my open hands, remembering the strange gesture he had made. It was something familiar and foreign at the same time.

"Finley, look!" Aiby exclaimed. "Apparently there is a way to identify a Green Man!"

I saw she was pointing at the last paper. "But how?" I asked.

Aiby jumped off the floor and scurried over to *The Big Book of Magical Objects*. "We have to use the Sherwood Compass."

"But how?" I repeated. "And what is that?"

"I don't know," Aiby said. "Which means we don't have it here in the shop."

Intrigued, I watched Aiby page through the *BBMO*. "Here it is!" she said. "Sherwood's Compass." She put a finger on the page and began to slide it down the rows of the spell.

"Is there only one book about magical items?" I asked.

"What do you mean?" she asked.

"I mean, do you pass this book from one family to another, or does each family have a different book?"

"There is only one book," Aiby said, reading. "And

every time the family closes shop, they deliver the book to the next family. This is interesting — take a look." Aiby showed me a few lines of the spell. "We have to check in a book called the *Grand Register of Sightings*, but apparently the only Sherwood Compass that still exists is located right here in Applecross."

"That can't be a coincidence," I said.

"Of course not," Aiby said.

"Was it your grandfather's?" I asked, remembering Aiby's ancestor. He'd been shipwrecked under mysterious circumstances in the bay, which eventually took his name, Reginald.

"No," Aiby said. "In fact, it's even stranger. Apparently the Sherwood Compass belongs to the McBlack family."

I jumped. "The McBlacks?!"

Aiby ignored me and continued reading. I thought back to Barragh McBlack, the man I'd heard arguing with my father the day before. There were lots of rumors about him, and most people said it was better to just avoid the McBlacks, as well as their so-called Scary Villa.

A ringing noise startled me. "What's that?" I asked.

Aiby handed me the book and walked to the window. "Keep reading, jumpy," she said, a mischievous smile dancing on her lips. "Someone's at the door."

I looked down at the open pages of the *BBMO*. The passage described a weather vane topped with a tin-plated dragon. I reached a point in the passage where the writing flickered before my eyes like tadpoles in a puddle. I realized it was the Enchanted Language. I tried to read some of it, but I couldn't understand much.

"Need some help?" Aiby asked, startling me.

"No, thanks, I read it all just fine," I lied. "Um, who was at the door?"

"The person we need right now," Aiby said.

"Huh? Need for what?" I asked.

"Transportation to Scary Villa," she said, taking the *BBMO* from my hands. "If you want to find the Green Man, then we have to find the Sherwood Compass first. And to find the Sherwood Compass . . ."

A familiar voice called Aiby's name from outside the shop. My eyes went wide. "Doug?" I asked, fighting back a wave of anger. "What is my brother doing here? He should be working at the farm!"

"And you should be working at the beach, if I'm not mistaken," Aiby said.

"Yeah, but . . . that's different!" I insisted.

Aiby shrugged. "Not really."

She had a point. So I went outside to face my brother.

JACK'S MAGIC BEANS

ENCHANTED EMPORIUM

Once planted, these beans exhibit different magical powers depending on their color. Green beans grow into mystical fairy plants. Yellow beans attract geese that lay golden eggs. Black beans stop the sun from moving for eighteen minutes. Once swallowed, the purple beans force you to tell the truth for seven weeks.

Chapter
THIRTEEN

SECRET DOORS,
DEMONIC DOGS,
& MAGICAL FLUTES

At just past noon, Reginald Bay looked as still and reflective as a mirror. Mr. Dogberry's boat motor spat out puffs of smoke as it sliced through the otherwise motionless water. I glanced back at the coast, astonished by how different it looked from way out here.

Doug sat at the stern, controlling the motor by hand. He was gifted at using mechanical things, but I'd never tell him that. Aiby was seated at the bow, her legs crossed like a happy spider, seemingly enjoying the wind in her hair. In the middle of the boat, beneath Patches, was Aiby's bag. She'd packed our lunches inside it, but I was pretty sure there was a magical object or two in there, as well.

From time to time, Doug threw me an awkward glance that seemed to say, "We'll talk later, face to face." I gulped.

After Aiby had explained to Doug that we wanted to leave for Scary Villa as soon as possible, Doug said that didn't seem like a good idea. Aiby acted annoyed and made a few complaints, which quickly changed Doug's mind. From watching her manipulate Doug, I realized she'd used the same trick on me many times before. A good lesson for me to learn, I guess.

Anyway, a little after 1 p.m. we reached a landing stone that had been eroded by the sea. It had two fraying ropes attached to it that led to the carcasses of two rotten boats. Doug slowed the boat while I moved to the side and prepared to jump onto the rock. A minute later, we were successfully moored.

We climbed up a path that had been invaded by weeds. Clearly no one had visited for many years. The trail eventually led to a grassy clearing full of white flowers that waved in the wind. I almost tripped several times because of the many mole holes. We passed a couple of boulders and eventually reached a dirt road that was dotted with holes.

We soon arrived at Scary Villa's front gate. The gate's black, pointy bars blocked passage to the two driveways beyond it. On each side of the gate was one continuous brick wall that surrounded the entire property. The yard itself was dotted with low trees and surrounded by a strange mist that the summer sun couldn't quite seem to penetrate.

"Is 'Scary Villa' the house's real name?" Aiby asked.

"Nah," Doug said. "It's just the nickname the villagers gave it when the creepy McBlack family moved in. It's original name was Carolina Villa, or something."

"Either way, we need to be careful," I added. "People say a lot of stupid, unbelievable things about this house, but one thing is true." Aiby tried to interrupt me, but I gestured for her to wait. "I've been here once before, after I took over Jules's mail route . . ."

I pointed at the mailbox, which for some reason was located on the other side of the closed gate. No one could reach it from the outside, including mailmen.

"Jules told me he just stops at the gate, slips any mail he has for the McBlacks through the bars, then leaves," I said. I pointed at a small, metal chain hanging down from the gate. "You see that small chain there?"

They nodded.

"Well, the chain opens the gate just enough to reach the mailbox. But you have to be fast, because as soon as you touch the chain, Cromwell comes running."

Patches's hair stood on end when heard the big black dog's name. "I can't tell you exactly what kind of dog Cromwell is, but he's huge. He has creepy yellow eyes and his barks are so sharp and loud that they'll make your blood run cold."

Doug didn't look impressed. "If you're fast enough to deliver the mail," I said, "then you can get back to the other side of the gate before Cromwell gets you."

Doug snorted. "Oooh, that sounds so scary!" he said. "So where's this demonic dog, anyway? He's not out in the yard, so what's the big problem?"

"You won't see him until you pull the chain," I said. "But rest assured, once you do, Cromwell will come running."

"Well let's summon this Cromwell, then!" Doug said, approaching the chain. Patches barked.

"Doug, are you crazy?" I cried. "We can't just do that!"

"Then what's the plan," Doug said flatly.

"The plan is simple," I said. "We enter secretly, recover the Sherwood Compass, and escape before the McBlacks even notice we're here."

"So we're going to steal something," Doug said.

"Not really," Aiby said. "In *The Big Book of Magical Objects*, the notes for the Sherwood Compass state that the McBlacks never paid for it. And payment on purchase is one of the three basic rules of the shop."

Doug smirked. "So we're more like repo men than thieves?" Doug said. "I'm cool with that. But why do we want this compass, anyway?"

"Because it is the only magical object in existence that can help us locate a Green Man," I said.

Doug raised an eyebrow at me. "You mean, the thing you said you saw at the end of the lawn at our house?" he said. "You think he made all the sheep disappear?"

I nodded.

Doug shifted his weight to one leg. "So is this Green Man dangerous?" he asked.

I shrugged and glanced at Aiby. I hadn't really considered if this Green Man was a threat to us. Now I was even more worried about what we were getting ourselves into.

"We have to find out who he is, why he came to Applecross, and what he wants," Aiby said. "It's the only way to fix Applecross's problems. But in order to find the Sherwood Compass . . ." Aiby pointed at the brick wall, then shrugged.

We began to walk along the gate, studying the wall in search of the best place to climb. "Do you have a magical bone that makes dogs fall sleep?" I asked Aiby.

"Nope," Aiby said. "But don't worry, I have something in mind that will help us deal with Cromwell."

"Really?" I said. "Mind sharing?"

Aiby just kept walking. *I guess now's not the time for that question, either,* I thought. Insects buzzed around us until a gentle breeze from the sea blew by. Some of the leaves on the nearby trees fell to the ground.

I wondered when exactly the sleepy Scottish countryside had transformed into a twisted amusement park where my life was constantly at risk. It seemed so strange that a touch of magic could change everything.

"There," Aiby said, pointing at a part of the wall that was a bit lower than the rest.

I looked around. Behind us, the land was flat. The nearest tree was about twenty feet from the wall, which was too far away to use to climb over the barrier.

Aiby dropped her bag on the ground and rifled through it. I didn't know what her plan was, but she seemed completely confident in it. Then again, while her self-confidence was her greatest virtue, it was also her greatest weakness. She always acted like she knew exactly what she was doing — even when she didn't.

I approached her and peeked over her shoulder. The bag was completely empty inside, yet she continued to rummage through it. "Hey, Aiby," I said. "Sorry to

interrupt, but could you possibly tell us what the heck we're going to do?"

She winked at me. "I'm looking for what we need," she said, then continued digging.

"Of course," I muttered. "Can you at least tell me why you're rummaging through an empty bag?"

Aiby snorted. "It's far from empty, Finley," she said. "This is a Bag of Darkness. It's super useful if you have to store a lot of things, especially when you don't know what you'll need on an adventure. It's a lot like the pockets in that pair of pants you loved too much to let go of." She giggled.

I snorted. "Very funny, Aiby."

"Ah, here it is!" Aiby said. She pulled out a leather case, opened it, and pulled out a piece of white chalk. Then she began to rummage through the bag again. A moment later, she produced a long, golden flute.

"Chalk and a flute? That's our plan?" Doug said, massaging his temples. "I am so confused right now."

"Doug, you told me the other day that you have a passion for music," Aiby said.

I chuckled. As far as I knew, the only music my brother liked was the sound of his own name being cheered by a chorus of fans at the rugby field.

Doug looked at the flute. "Of course, Aiby, but —"

"I'll explain, don't worry," she said, handing him the flute.

Aiby faced the brick wall. She drew a vertical line with the chalk. Then she drew a second, parallel line about three feet away from the first. Finally, she joined the two lines at the top with a third line. Once the rectangle of a door was drawn, Aiby drew a small knob.

Aiby took a step back and pressed lightly on the wall. The chalk-drawn portion of the wall opened toward us like a door! Doug and I were speechless, but Patches wasn't afraid. He gave out a brave little bark and casually trotted through the opening.

Aiby glanced at Doug. "This is the Golden Flute of Hamelin. Have you heard of the tale of the Pied Piper? He began to play his flute, and anyone he thought of was helplessly compelled to follow him. So, after Finley and I go through, you can go wherever you want on this side of the wall — just make sure you do three things: keep thinking of Cromwell, keep moving, and keep playing the flute."

Doug frowned. "How long should I keep doing that?"

A wild howl came from the McBlack yard, followed by a tiny but furious bark. Aiby pushed me through the opening. "Hurry up, Doug!" she said. "Start playing!"

That's when we saw Cromwell running toward us

in a black blur. For a second, it looked like Doug was going to run, but he managed to compose himself and lifted the flute to his mouth. Aiby crouched on her knees, grabbed Patches by the scruff of his neck, and moved away from the door. Patches kept running in the air as Aiby held him.

Just then, a black mountain of hair leaped right past us and through the door with terrifying speed — right at Doug.

I heard a faint series of off-key notes being played on the other side of the wall as Aiby jumped to her feat. "Now!" she cried.

In a flash, Aiby pressed the other side of the magic door and closed it behind us, leaving that infernal beast on the other side of the wall . . . with my brother.

"Doug!" I cried, slamming my fists against the wall. I turned to glare at Aiby. "What have we done to him?!"

"Don't worry!" Aiby said. "The melody of that flute has the power to soothe even the fiercest beast. Cromwell will follow Doug wherever he goes. As long as your brother keeps playing and walking, he'll be just fine."

I breathed a sigh of relief, although a tiny part of me was snickering on the inside. "I hope he doesn't faint or something," I said.

"Your brother will handle it just fine," she said. "Just listen: the barking has already stopped."

It was true. There was no sign of that demonic dog's blood-curdling howls.

Patches, on the other hand, was snarling at the magical door. I reached down to pet him. "It's okay, boy. I know you could've taken him." Patches gave out a little bark, then raised his hind leg against the wall and relieved himself.

Aiby squinted. "Dogs are weird."

"Yeah," I said. "Anyway, let's go."

As soon as I turned around, I realized we weren't alone. A crowd of people were standing in the garden — and they were staring right at us.

BAG OF DARKNESS

Bags of Darkness come in many shapes and sizes, but this particular one resembles a doctor's bag. This incredibly useful magical object can hold countless items of any size and shape. Once deposited into the bag, items can be retrieved if marked with a Fermacose (see page 142) or with a lot of luck.

ENCHANTED
EMPORIUM

Chapter
FOURTEEN

THE MCBLACKS, MONTECRISTO, & SOMERLED

I couldn't move. I just kept staring wide-eyed at those motionless figures in the garden. They stood there, watching us, posed in impossible positions. It took me a long while to realize they were just statues.

I'd heard that Barragh McBlack had a collection of strange statues, but I hadn't expected them to be so . . . creepy. There were men with octopus heads, ducks with wheels for legs, and giant shrimp with glowing gemstones for eyes. Sure, they were bizarre and terrifying, but I had to admit they were pretty interesting, too.

Aiby and I exchanged glances, then headed toward the house. As we neared Scary Villa, we reached the first of those monstrous statues.

"It's made of porcelain," Aiby said. She passed her

hand over a statue of a bug-eyed child wearing a shiny coat made of purple leather. "Creepy."

"Agreed," I said. The statues looked like they could come alive at any moment. "And very lifelike," I added, nearly unable to pull my eyes away.

We kept moving. Whenever we heard a noise, we stopped and ducked. For some reason, there was a golf hole with flag number 17 sticking out of it.

"Can I ask you something, Aiby?" I asked.

"Sure."

"You know where the compass is, right?"

"More or less, yes," she said. "You read the entry in the *BBMO* too, right?"

"Err, yes, I sure did," I said. "I just wanted to make sure we're on the same page."

Aiby frowned at me. "Sherwood's Compass is more like a weather vane," she said.

I nodded. That much I knew from looking at the drawing. "So where will we look for it?"

"Well, they don't keep it inside the house, as you read."

"Of course," I said.

"So it should be somewhere out here, or in the barn," Aiby said.

We divided the garden between us and searched for

it for about ten minutes. Neither of us found anything related to Sherwood's Compass.

We walked toward the house and peered inside a window. It looked like no one was home. We examined the three front dormer windows, but saw nothing.

Aiby pointed at the barn. With great caution, we drew closer to a window on the barn's northern side. On top of the barn was a tall, wooden tower with a tin-plated roof. As we peered inside the window, we saw that part of the barn was being used as a pottery workshop. I saw the gaping mouth of a kiln, little dishes and pieces of statues on a small table, china pots, lumps of moist clay, molds of various shapes, and designs and drawings on the walls.

"Welcome to pack rat heaven," I whispered. "If the compass is inside there, we'll never find it."

"I don't think it is," Aiby said.

"Why is that?" I asked.

"Because of the oven," she said. "The intense heat would destroy the compass."

I smiled to hide my confusion. Maybe I should have tried harder to learn to read the Enchanted Language . . . or, you know, just admit to Aiby that I hadn't.

Heading toward the barn, we reached the side that had been converted into a garage. It had no windows, so

we risked pulling open the door to take a peek inside. I saw a long, black car that looked like a hearse. Next to it were tire marks from a second car. "At least we know that Barragh McBlack isn't home," I said.

We entered the garage. I locked the latch on the inside and started looking around. "Could it be in here?" I asked.

Aiby didn't answer me. She was examining a small puddle of fuel that was dripping from a tank on a shelf. I took a closer look at the car. It only had two seats in front, and the rear of the vehicle was equipped with sliding contraptions and covered by a sheet. Strangely, the car was full of dirt.

Patches growled. I turned to see he'd found one of those weird statues right behind the car still partially packed. It looked like a chubby girl with a pair of tentacles instead of legs. She had big, open eyes, long eyelashes, and a mole on her left cheek. She was wearing a blue dress and holding a beetle in her hand.

"So weird," I muttered. There was a sort of sad, hopeless melancholy to the statues of Scary Villa. It looked like they wanted to be left alone, which for some reason made them seem even more frightening.

In our search, we found a hedge trimmer, a farm tractor's engine, two headboards made of iron, about

twenty doors and windows stacked against the walls, and several pieces of unrecognizable machinery.

But no sign of a weather vane.

We ventured deeper into the garage, making our way through endless cobwebs and clouds of dust that proved no one had been that far back in the garage in ages. At the opposite side of the barn, we found a wooden ladder built into the wall.

"Do you think the compass is up there?" I asked.

Aiby pointed at a hatch in the ceiling. A weird piece of metal was attached to the handle that looked like a cross between a fancy piece of decorative metalwork and a complex lock. "That's where I'd keep something I wouldn't want anyone to find," she said.

"Hm," I said. "That lock does look a little out of place in a dumpy garage like this."

Aiby nodded. She tested the lower rungs of the ladder with her foot, then climbed up high enough to touch the lock. "It's more complex than I imagined."

"What do you mean?" I asked.

"If my father were here, he would know precisely who made this contraption, and why," she said. "But I can't identify it." She placed her finger on one of the iron rivets and it moved, springing a gear. "However, it is definitely a magical lock of some kind."

"Surprise, surprise," I said, not at all surprised. "So now what?"

Aiby glanced down at me. "Now you have to find a way to open it."

"Like a key?" I asked.

She chuckled. "I don't think so. This lock is probably a Montecristo. If that's the case, then a key would be useless." She pointed to the various parts that made up the mechanism. "Each of these is like a letter. You just have to know where to move them and in what combination. Then it will open for you."

"So . . . we need a password?" I asked.

"No," she said with a smirk. "We need a *key*word."

"Ha, ha," I said. "Try 'bad luck.'"

"Very funny." Aiby pushed the mechanisms. They moved like an iron snake, but didn't open the lock.

"'Open sesame?'" I said. "'None shall pass?'"

"Can you please stop?" Aiby said. "You're making me nervous."

"Sorry," I said. I was also nervous. Sneaking around like a thief, hanging out with an octopus-girl in a blue dress, examining a hearse, and hoping your brother isn't being eaten by a monstrous dog will do that to you.

Tick, tack! Tick, tack! went the noisy lock as Aiby manipulated it.

I went back to the entrance and peered through the cracks in the boards. Seen from this side, the ivy-covered walls of Scary Villa didn't look so terrible. Compared to the room we were in now, it was a ray of sunshine. The shadow of the barn and its tower was projected onto the lawn in front of me.

Tick, tack! Tick, tack! Aiby worked the lock.

One by one, I examined the windows of the house. It didn't just look empty — it seemed abandoned. How many family members did Barragh McBlack have? Was he married? Did he have any children? And how old was he? I realized I didn't know anything about them — when they'd move to Applecross, how they'd come into possession of a magical object, or anything. Did they even know it was magical? Maybe Barragh knew more than he seemed to about the odd events in Applecross.

I thought again about old lady Cumai's death and how I'd missed the opportunity to speak to her one last time. Before Aiby and her family had arrived, I'd thought I'd known everything about Applecross. Now I realized I knew nothing. For example, there was a mill at Applecross, but when had there ever been wheat growing here to grind?

"Forget it!" Aiby cried from the opposite side of the garage. "Without the right keyword, it'll never open."

"Maybe we could ask Barragh when he returns home," I said.

"He wouldn't tell us," she said. "Dad isn't . . . friendly with him."

"They know each other?" I asked.

"Their great-grandparents knew each other," she said. "Way back when the McBlacks took the Compass without paying for it."

I tapped my chin. "Have you tried 'horror' as the keyword?"

"Not funny," Aiby said.

"I'm not joking," I said. "Horror is how I'd describe this place. Horror, fear, that kind of thing."

I examined the front of the statue for clues. Eventually, I saw something I'd previously missed: there was a signature painted on the statue's base. I figured I'd find Barragh McBlack's name, but instead it read: *Somerled McBlack*.

I turned to Aiby, who was still on the top rung staring at the lock. "Hey, Aiby."

"What?"

"Somerled. Try the word 'Somerled' with that lock."

Aiby shrugged, then began to fiddle with the mechanism.

Tick, tack, TOCK!

Aiby beamed at me. "Finley, it worked!"

I winked and followed my friend up the ladder.

The top floor of the tower had become a refuge for birds. The floor, half-covered by a large Oriental carpet, was blanketed in bird poop. I glanced up to see one of the skylights had broken. Aiby and I rifled through the many objects abandoned there. After examining several chests and drawers, we realized the compass wasn't there.

"Maybe the birds took it," I said. "Or maybe your system of recording the locations of magical objects isn't as accurate as you think."

Aiby didn't respond. She just kept tossing boxes aside and opening trunks. Looking out the west-facing skylight, I saw no trace of Doug or Cromwell. I hoped that nothing bad had happened to my brother.

Through another skylight, I saw the pale sun of the early afternoon cast the barn's shadow on the lawn below. My eyes went wide. "Come here for a minute, Aiby," I whispered.

My friend joined me. "Did you find it?"

I pointed to the shadow below us. On top of the tower's shadow was the shape of a weather vane.

I grinned at Aiby. "Maybe the McBlack family just used the Sherwood Compass as a normal weather vane."

Aiby returned my grin. "Let's go find out," she said.

Finder's Case

Inside this mysterious case is a special pouch that holds several pieces of magical chalk. Each colored piece has a unique enchantment. The white one allows the user to create functional doors on walls, ceilings, or floors. The red one gives inanimate objects the gift of speech. The yellow one attracts birds. Lastly, the black chalk is a Fermacose, which can be used to mark objects placed inside a Bag of Darkness for easy retrieval (see page 131).

Chapter
FIFTEEN

A COMPASS,
BIRD POOP,
& GEMSTONE EYES

I've climbed my own roof many times, so I figured climbing the McBlack's barn roof wouldn't be much different. Boy was I wrong. Instead of just climbing out my bedroom window, I had to crawl through a broken skylight covered in bird poop and pull myself up onto a narrow ledge.

You're probably saying I'm crazy, but if you were the defender of the Enchanted Emporium, and you were with a girl like Aiby Lily, then I think you'd have done the same thing I did. I mean, I could've made up a dozen excuses or alternatives, but it wouldn't have mattered. I just couldn't say no to her.

So there I was, on the roof of the barn, with my torn

shirt and scratched hands. Normally I would've been scared stiff by the height, but it didn't compare much to my earlier adventure that week with Aiby's father on that ridiculous wall.

I crawled across the roof on my stomach, doing my best to ignore the blustery wind. Crows buzzed overhead and cawed noisily, apparently annoyed by my invasion of their territory.

The tin roof was scorchingly hot. It felt like my butt was resting on my dad's tractor's engine at the end of a long day of farming. After a few minutes of scooting along like a gecko across hot sand, I spotted the weather vane. It was little more than a pole with a tin-plated dragon on the top.

I did my best to push down my fear of falling and crawled to the top. Easing off my butt, I stood and grabbed the base of the vane. I pulled it, but it didn't come free.

I yanked the weather vane a second time, then a third, but it wouldn't budge. I was getting frustrated, and the familiar soft voice in the back of my head advised me to give up and get down from the roof. Instead, I put all my weight behind one final pull.

The base cracked and it came free — and I dropped the weather vane! With a dive a gymnast would be

jealous of, I grabbed it just before it tumbled off the edge of the roof. As I grabbed it, the tip of the weather vane sliced my finger.

"Ouch!" I cried. For some reason, it burned like fire. I checked the cut. It was small, probably no larger than a paper cut, which relieved me a bit.

That was a close one, I thought. I lay on my back and closed my eyes. I could hear the magic flute's subtle, off-key notes in the distance.

Good job, Finley, I told myself. *Now it's time to get off this stupid roof.* I took in a deep breath and opened my eyes. Lazy clouds hovered above me. I exhaled, then rolled over onto my stomach.

That's when I saw her. I blinked hard to make sure I wasn't imagining things. Twenty yards away, in one of the big windows of Scary Villa, I saw a girl. She was definitely watching me. Judging by the curious look on her face, she must have observed my crazy climb and my theft of the weather vane. She was pale, with big eyes and a tiny mouth. She looked to be about my age, or maybe a year or two older. I recognized the same sad look in her that I'd seen in the statue in the garage.

Our eyes were locked. Neither of us moved or spoke, like two funny birds on the roofs of their respective homes.

Then, for some reason, I waved at her. "Hello, Somerled," I called out. I pointed to my chest and added, "I'm Finley — with an 'F.'"

For a few seconds, Somerled did nothing. She just stood with her face pressed against the window, making pancakes of her pale cheeks as they squished against the glass.

I raised the weather vane up and then pointed at my wrist where a watch would be. I was trying to say, *I need this for a little while, but I will bring it back to you when I'm done.*

Amazingly, she seemed to understand. She smiled and nodded. I gave her a thumbs-up until Somerled raised hers as well. She seemed to be saying, *Go ahead and take it, Finley McPhee. Just make sure to bring it back.*

Then she stepped away from the window, turned around, and quickly ran out of sight.

A few moments later, I scurried off the barn's roof with the clatter of a thousand marching drums. Thankfully, Aiby grabbed my legs and dragged me in through the skylight. She asked me if I was injured, and I told her that I was fine since I'd already forgotten about the cut on my finger.

"I've seen Somerled," I said.

"And who is Somerled?" she asked.

"Barragh McBlack's daughter, I think. And she saw me."

Aiby brushed my jeans off. "Then we'd better get out of here," she said.

"She wasn't angry," I said. "She even smiled at me."

"Either way, we have to leave."

I nodded. We climbed down the ladder and reached the door. I glanced back at the statue of the little girl with the tentacles. "I think those statues were made by Somerled," I said.

Aiby frowned. "Then I don't want to meet her," she said.

We ran from the barn back to the wall where Aiby had drawn the magical door. Once there, she knocked on the wall, and the door opened. When Doug saw us, we watched as he led Cromwell back through the door like some mythical beast. Once they were through, Doug jumped back through to our side and Aiby quickly closed the magic door behind him.

"It's about time!" Doug cried, removing the flute from his lips.

Aiby showed him the weather vane. "Mission accomplished," she said.

"And now that you have it, what's your plan?" Doug asked.

The Golden Flute of Hamelin

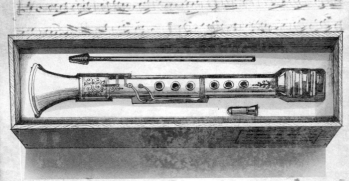

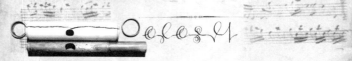

Cast from the same bar of gold as the
first pure gold currency in Venice, Italy, this
enchanted flute has the power to charm anyone
who hears its melody. Once charmed, listeners
must follow the player wherever he or she goes.
The only way to resist the flute's enchanting
melody is through the use of Magical Earplugs.

Aiby explained our plan to Doug as we walked toward the path that led down to the bay. She and Doug led the way while I brought up the rear.

"Doug, did you know that Barragh McBlack has a daughter?" I asked him.

"No," he answered. "Is she pretty?"

I had to think about that for a moment. I recalled the creepy statues that she'd made, and felt a cold shiver run down my spine. Sure, she was beautiful . . . but in a way, so are ghosts.

In a soft voice, I told my brother, "No. I would have to say no."

Doug chuckled. "That's why I haven't heard of her," he said.

Typical Doug, I thought. At that moment, I decided something: no matter what happened tomorrow, the most important thing I'd do would be returning the weather vane to Somerled.

And maybe talk to her a little.

We reached the dock and jumped into the boat. I was so absorbed in my thoughts that I hardly noticed a sparkle just below the water's surface. I leaned over the edge of the boat and saw one of Somerled's statues staring back at me with childlike, gemstone eyes.

Chapter
SIXTEEN

THE WOODS,
VOICES,
& THE DEAD

Later, after returning from Scary Villa, I learned that some strange events had transpired while we were gone. Apparently, two more sheep had disappeared, so Professor Everett gave his hunting rifle to the night patrol. Apparently it was a special rifle that used silver bullets, which was weird for a variety of reasons. Mostly I just wondered why Professor Everett owned a gun that was designed to kill werewolves.

At a town meeting, my father shared new evidence he'd found of this cattle thief: an empty bottle of whiskey.

"It is one of the best whiskeys, Camas," Mr. McStay said. As the owner of the McStay Inn, he was an expert on buying (and drinking) whiskey. Mrs. Greenlock, the owner of the local pub, nodded in agreement.

Dad explained that he'd found it the previous night in front of the door to his house — the same time he'd called out to me, preventing me from following the Green Man into the woods. "Does anything about this bottle strike any of you as strange?" he asked the group.

"Well, it's a little odd that a sheep thief would drink expensive Scottish whiskey," someone answered.

"I only had three bottles of it," said Mrs. Greenlock. "Two of them were purchased by a customer, but I still have the third one."

"Who bought the two bottles?" Jules asked from inside his red van.

"A man I'd never seen before," she said.

"Do you mean Locan Lily?" Barragh suggested.

"No, not him," Ms. Greenlock said. "A young man. He was a tourist. He said he was renting a cottage on the coast and liked to go for morning jogs. Did any of you see someone jogging on the beaches recently?"

The men shrugged and shook their heads.

"That's a shame," my father said. "It could be an important link."

And it was. None of us could have imagined that the young man who had arrived in Applecross to go jogging on the beaches during the day was also wandering the forests at night, wrapped in a Cloak of Mirrors. At that point in time, there was no way to know that he was studying the area, waiting for the perfect time to strike. His name was Semueld — and if he had left an empty whiskey bottle in front of our door, he had a good reason for doing so.

The crowd began to disperse and head home. "Man, I'm completely exhausted," I said. While we'd had a long day of walking, I was surprised at how tired I was.

"Quit complaining, Viper," Doug said, using my most hated nickname. "I'm fine, and I'm the one carried the boat to the dock."

Before I could respond, he whispered something to Aiby, then walked away.

"What did he say?" I asked after he'd left.

"He said, 'Maybe I'll see you later in the country,'" she said.

* * *

A little while later, Aiby headed up the Emporium's steps with the compass in hand. I slowly trudged behind her, my legs feeling like concrete blocks.

As we entered the shop, Aiby greeted her father and showed him the compass.

Mr. Lily looked concerned. "If that thing works, then we'll know for sure that this isn't just a case of some weirdo wandering around in the woods at night," he said.

Aiby nodded grimly.

A few minutes later, we both stood outside the shop again. "So, let's begin the hunt!" she said.

Aiby held a couple of books in her hands, on top of which was a Mythic Thermometer. Aiby said it analyzed the magical potential of certain objects.

She held the device over our Sherwood Compass and the small rod on the Mythic Thermometer shot up to level 13 of 21.

"Awesome!" Aiby cried out in relief. "It works!"

I suddenly realized that I had risked my life to steal a magical object that might not have even worked. But when I saw that determined sparkle in Aiby's eyes, I couldn't help but think that I'd made the right choice.

"Isn't it exciting?" Aiby asked. "I mean, we just recovered the weather vane that Robin Hood used to earn the friendship of the men of Sherwood Forest!"

I nodded. Aiby took my hand and walked back to my bike with me. I hopped on, then she sat on the handlebars while I pedaled. As we headed back to Applecross, she explained the entire plan to me while Patches trotted happily behind us.

From time to time, while explaining the plan, Aiby

let go of the handlebars to gesture as she always did, which meant I had to adjust quickly so she wouldn't fall off.

"Sorry!" she told me each time.

"No problem," I answered each time.

Between Aiby's musical voice, the scent of grass coming from Balanch Ba, the gentle sound of waves, and Aiby's hair tickling my face, I'd never been happier. As we passed old lady Cumai's mill, I noticed that all the lights were on, just as Barragh McBlack had said.

A few minutes later, we arrived at Professor Everett's gift shop. As usual, he was sitting outside and shuffling the strange deck of grimy cards he used to play solitaire all day long.

Aiby asked him if he had a map of the peninsula's paths, and the two of them entered the store to get one. When they returned, the Professor sat down and continued to play with his cards. "Are you done testing those beaches?" he asked me.

"Almost, Professor," I lied. To disguise my lie, I casually crushed a beetle under my shoe.

We listened as the church bells rang five times, then we left. A couple of minutes later, we reached Meb's dress shop.

"Is anyone here?" Aiby asked, pushing open the door.

"Hey you two!" Meb said.

Aiby quickly explained to Meb what our plan was. The young dressmaker grabbed the keys to her tiny car, turned the sign on the shop's door from *OPEN* to *CLOSED*, and followed us out.

A moment later, we were off. As we passed the mill, Meb said, "Someone should go turn those lights off." But she didn't stop.

As always, I was sitting in the back with Patches and watching the scenery fly by. Aiby continually checked her map. "Go that way," she'd say, pointing.

Meb soon left the coastal road and turned onto the dangerous single-lane road. We headed past the heart of the forest of Applecross toward the dam.

As Meb took the hairpin turns with ease, she mentioned what her friends had been telling her about the sheep thief. I saw her face through the rearview mirror, and it looked like she hadn't slept much lately.

"The ladies of Applecross, especially the older ones, all love their gossip," Meb said. "After that crazy Dutch visitor from a few weeks ago, every single patron of the McStay Inn has been thoroughly speculated about. Apparently, Aiby, your father is a topic of interest. The ladies say he wanders the land at night, traveling from one side of the countryside to the other."

"That's right," said Aiby. "But he's just searching for fallen trees to fix the steps that lead down to the sea from our shop."

"That's what I told them," Meb said. "But they refuse to stop gossiping. I sort of understand the concern, since so many strange things have happened since your family arrived in Applecross."

"Hmph," Aiby said without taking her eyes off the map.

"They also love to speculate where Mrs. Lily is, or why Aiby isn't enrolled in school," Meb continued. "I was hoping you could answer those questions for me so I could pass the information on to them so they would, you know . . . leave it be."

"I've already graduated from school," Aiby said quietly. Then, crinkling the map far more than necessary, she completely unfolded it so it took up most of the front of the car.

We stopped halfway up the hill and exited the car with the Sherwood Compass and the sandwiches we'd brought along for lunch. I wasn't all that hungry, so I split mine with Patches.

"Let's get started," Aiby said. She passed me the weather vane, then blindfolded me. With my eyes covered, she wrapped my hand around the base of the

weather vane and whispered the magical formula in my ear:

I lifted the blindfold enough to look at Aiby. "That's all I have to say?" I asked.

"Yes, but it takes a man to use this compass," she said. Coming from her mouth, that simple phrase filled me with pride.

I positioned myself at the edge of the road with my back facing Meb's car. Slowly, I pronounced the secret phrase. Immediately I felt the weather vane rotate as the dragon on top pointed in a new direction. That strange voice inside my head whispered a warning, *Remember what happened last time you messed with a monster?*

I felt the dragon lift upward five times, then stop. Aiby placed her hand on my shoulder. "Good work — we found something. The dragon reared up five times!"

"And that means . . . ?"

"We move forward five hundred yards in the direction it pointed," she said. "And then we do it over again."

★ ★ ★

Soon the sun began to set, turning the sea a golden hue. The island mountains in the distance cast shadows like castles against the curtain of coming night. We soon found ourselves lost in the thick forest, with Sherwood's Compass our only source of direction in the scant light. Each time the weather vane's dragon reared up, we followed where it pointed.

As we made our way through the trees, the smell of the wilderness grew stronger. I began to feel uneasy in the near total silence. The tree branches seemed to curve like dead fingers. The grass grew denser and more resistant to our footsteps. Every single stone was sharp and slippery.

The compass twisted in my hands as I repeated the incantation that tuned it to the magic that still remained in the world. But with each incantation, I felt weaker, as if pronouncing the string of words cost me some sort of spiritual energy.

Patches, though, was happy as ever, excited to explore the forest. Meb was a little worried about nightfall, but Aiby seemed completely focused on the task at hand.

"Are we sure that it works?" I asked for probably the twentieth time. We seemed to be zigzagging more than heading in a specific direction. While I realized that

magic often seemed to work outside the realm of logic, I still felt like we were heading nowhere.

"Yep," Aiby said. "Have a little patience, Fin. Not all magic works quickly."

"Can I ask you something?" I asked. "What does that spell I keep repeating even mean?"

"*Nature loves to hide,*" she answered.

"But those words, 'physis vattelapesca.' What language is that?"

"It's ancient Greek," she said.

"And why is it in ancient Greek?" I asked.

Aiby shrugged. "Maybe the magical object originally belonged to someone who loved ancient Greece?"

It was a fair answer, but not at all satisfying. I mean, what's the point of an incantation if you don't even know what the words mean? I decided I would study the Enchanted Language once this adventure was over.

"It was a language that was spoken many years ago," Aiby said. "These days, it would be considered a dead language. Like Latin."

We kept walking. The wind made her hair dance around her shoulders while her toes stepped through tufts of moss. As I watched her walk through the woods like a woman of the wild, it seemed like I'd known her for much longer than I had. Strange words wandered through my head, one after another, so fast that I had to stop and sit down.

Aiby and Meb stopped alongside me. "I don't really think languages can be considered dead, Aiby," Meb said. "They still exist, they just aren't used in casual conversation or by any specific cultures."

Aiby nodded. "Oh, I agree. I don't think there are dead people, either," Aiby said. Meb raised an eyebrow. "My mom used to say that life is eternal, and that dead people are simply the living who lost their curiosity of life."

That's beautiful, I thought. *Aiby sure has a way with words.*

Aiby turned and smiled at me, and for a moment I wondered if she could read my thoughts. Ridiculous, I know, but it sure would've explained a lot.

"Even when people die," she said, "they continue to talk to us, or ask us questions, kind of like a voice deep inside our minds."

"That happens to me all the time," I said. "Hearing a voice in my head, I mean. But I usually ignore it."

Meb laughed. "And whose voice is it?" she asked.

"What do you mean?" I asked.

"Whose voice do you hear in your head?" Meb repeated.

I was caught off-guard by the question, but I didn't hesitate. "My grandmother's, I think," I said.

I looked up at Aiby and something strange happened: her skin . . . quivered. Or maybe it was her aura, if you believe in that kind of thing. I'd never seen anything like that before, but on that afternoon, in the woods, my sense of perception seemed amplified.

"My grandmother died when I was seven," I said quietly.

Aiby nodded. "My mom —" Aiby began, but Patches began to bark furiously. Then he dashed away into the depths of the forest.

"Patches heard something," I said.

"I heard it, too," Aiby said.

"What is it?" I asked.

The skin on Aiby's arm seemed to shimmer with light. "Let's go see," she said.

SHERWOOD COMPASS

This magical compass was crafted from an arrow once used by an ancient Scottish people. The tip was coated in the Lifeblood of the Forest, so great care must be taken when handling it. The compass's original purpose was to highlight the passageways between the magical world (the World of the Others) and our own. The compass has been owned by Robin Hood, William Shakespeare, and Titania, Queen of the Fairies. Most recently, it was procured without payment by the McBlack family in Suffolk, England, and now resides with them in Applecross, Scotland.

Chapter
SEVENTEEN

FISH BONES,
A WEATHER VANE,
& BARLEY GRAINS

I realized we were on the right path when I saw the grass beneath my feet was singed. I couldn't decide if I was relieved or disappointed. The smell of the wild was also more intense, like it was part of the very air itself.

A few moments after his display of adventurousness, Patches returned. He started to yelp while leaping around my ankles. I pet him and continued onward.

I pushed aside some branches and found myself in front of a small cave, its entrance partially covered by woven branches. Immediately I recalled the story of the two green children we'd read about in *The Black Book of the Woods* . . .

We entered cautiously. Just inside the cave, there were three sheep tied to stakes.

"Mystery solved," Meb said.

"Not really," I said, looking around. The cave was small and shallow. "It's a dead end, and this cave is far too small to hold all the town's missing sheep."

Unless, I thought, *the cave has another entrance.* I tried to recall the whole story of those two green children. They'd lived somewhere else, then entered the cave and found themselves in a forest. The forest of Suffolk.

On the ground, I saw dozens of fish bones and a mountain of shrimp shells. The smell was unbearable, and clouds of flies were buzzing around both piles. Deeper inside the cave, some of the grass had been pressed down in the shape of a crude bed.

"Either way," Aiby said, "this seems to be the place our sheep thief lives."

"Lucky for us, he isn't home," I added.

Patches sniffed the air, his tail snapping back and forth like a whip.

"Yuck," Meb said, staring at the refuse. "We need to untie the sheep and tell the others about this place."

Not yet, I thought. I knelt in the grass, swatting away the flies with my palm. In the shells, I saw something strange that looked like small, elongated slivers of gold.

I took one between my fingers and rolled it between them. "Hey," I said. "This is a grain of barley."

Along with barley, shrimp shells, and fish bones, we

found a container with some hot peppers inside as well as a chipped whiskey bottle. It was the same brand of whiskey that Dad had found in front of our house.

Suddenly, a roar shook the forest. Patches jumped back and yelped.

"What was that?!" Aiby asked.

"It was a rifle shot!" I said.

We'd had enough for one day. The four of us ran through the woods in the general direction we'd come. The evening light stretched through the branches, casting shadows like long, dark fingers. By some miracle, we reached Meb's car just as the sun dipped below the horizon. I could already see the stars piercing the black veil of the night sky.

Aiby jumped into the front. I hopped in the back.

"Who fired that shot?" Aiby asked.

"And at whom?" Meb added, starting the car.

Aiby turned on the small dome light in the passenger side of the car and began to leaf through one of the two books she had in the car. I still felt weird, otherwise I would've teased Aiby for her habit of looking for answers in ancient books. I just felt too out of it to joke around.

"Now that I've seen where it lives," Aiby said, "I think I can find this creature of ours in *The Grand Book of Magical Creatures . . .*"

"Great," I muttered. "What are you searching for?"

"I checked the index for the words: sheep, fish, barley, and whiskey."

I laughed. It wasn't all that surprising, considering most magical encyclopedias were sorted by words or phrases. That way, magicians leafing through the volumes could find things relevant to their magical interests far more easily.

"Well? Did you find anything?" I asked.

"Maybe," Aiby said. "I'm not certain, but I think we're dealing with a wild being called a psychopomp."

Patches barked.

"Patches stole my question," I said. "What the heck is a psychopomp?"

"The psychopomps are like guides who accompany living beings from one world to another," she said. "Like Charon, the ferryman of souls, who shows the way for those who must leave this world."

"You mean the dead," I said.

"Like I said, I don't think people die," Aiby said. "Not in that way. In any case, the particular psychopomp we're dealing with is a type of Green Man called Green Jack, or Jack in the Green. Apparently, he guides individuals back and forth between the real world and the magical world. In order to summon him, you need sheep, shrimp, roasted barley, and a special whiskey distilled with twenty-one hot peppers."

"Those are all the things we found in his lair," whispered Meb.

I saw the town's lights in the distance. "So someone has summoned him already?" I asked. "To do what?"

"The book says that Green Jack is considered to be extremely dangerous and uncooperative," Aiby said.

"Sounds about right, considering his love of whiskey," I said.

Aiby ignored my joke. "He lives barefoot, his feet are constantly burning . . ."

"That explains the burnt grass!" I said.

Aiby nodded. "And he loves to dress with long colorful cloaks and often wears a pair of black glasses with one broken lens. The broken lens lets him see the magical world while the other lens lets him see ours."

"A broken lens . . ." I said, trailing off. A detail popped into my head that had previously seemed unimportant. When I'd seen that strange man at the edge of my yard, I noticed a reflection of light in his face . . . as if he were wearing a pair of glasses with a broken lens!

"Stop the car!" I cried.

Meb shrugged, then slowed to a stop. I grabbed her and Aiby by their shoulders. "It was definitely him,"

I whispered. "When I saw him, he was making this strange gesture with his hands, like . . . well I can't really explain it. But he kept doing it, over and over."

Aiby scratched her chin and continued to read. "Apparently, whenever Green Jack is seen in an area, one person dies each week for three weeks."

"Three weeks?" I said. "So, twenty-one days."

"Like twenty-one hot peppers," Meb added.

I shivered. "Twenty-one grams," I added. "The weight of the soul." Aiby raised an eyebrow at me. "Um, I heard it in a movie Doug was watching."

Aiby shrugged. "The book says that Green Jack finds his victims by examining them with his glasses. If a person looks interesting enough through both lenses —"

"What do you mean by 'interesting?'" I asked.

Aiby turned the page. "Magic Soul," she said. "If a person has a Magic Soul, then he challenges them."

"Challenges them to what?" I asked quietly.

Aiby frowned. "It says 'a simple card game.' If Green Jack wins, he takes the person's Magic Soul for himself."

"And if Green Jack loses?" I asked.

"The book says that he has never lost."

I sank deeper into my seat. "But what kind of simple card game?" I asked.

Aiby slammed the book shut. I wasn't sure if that

meant there were no more answers, or if she didn't like the thought of playing games with Green Jack.

Soon, we arrived in Applecross. The street lamps were lit, and countless moths were flitting around the halos of light. "We have to warn the others," I said. "And find a way to stop this guy."

"How?" Aiby asked. "We just give him a call and ask him to leave?"

I shrugged. "How long have sheep been disappearing from Applecross?"

"For at least two weeks," Meb said.

"So, it started about the same time that old lady Cumai died." I said. "But then what? Mr. Dogberry died too, but long before any of this stuff started happening."

"What if Green Jack comes after one of us next?" Aiby said quietly.

"If he does, then we play his game," I said, smiling. "I volunteer — I have lots of good luck, after all."

Aiby shook her head but said nothing.

We parked in front of the Greenlock Pub and knew that something was wrong. As soon as the crowd saw us approaching, they ran toward us. They seemed agitated, but had every right to be.

"Someone shot Aiby's father."

Chapter
EIGHTEEN

THE GREEN MAN, SILVER BULLETS, & BLACKJACK

Aiby's shoulders slumped. I tried to support her in case she fainted. The three of us pushed through the crowd, but I lost sight of them. The last thing I saw was Meb making her way into the Greenlock Pub before I was overwhelmed by my neighbors.

"He was shot in Reginald Bay!" one man said.

"No! It was on the road leading to the bay!" another argued.

"It was the McBlacks, I tell you!" another man cried. "Mr. Lily was shot by Barragh!"

In a haze, I soon learned that Barragh McBlack had shot Mr. Lily somewhere on the road that led to Scary Villa during the night patrol. Upon realizing who he had shot, Barragh immediately drove Locan to the pub.

"But why did he bring Mr. Lily to the pub?" I asked. The villagers were crowded under the pub's banner depicting a green padlock.

"It was the only place where there was sure to be alcohol — you know, for disinfectant," Mr. Humpty Wallace explained, simultaneously wiping the beer foam from his mustache.

Another man nodded. "It was just the best thing to do."

"I was with Barragh on patrol," a man said. "There were two people on the road when he fired his rifle!"

"And Barragh shot one of them."

"The wrong one!"

"Are you sure of that?"

I had finally reached the pub's entrance when I heard a familiar voice. "Hey, McPhee," someone said. I turned to see Sammy Monkfish perched on a stool just outside the door. "What are you doing here?"

My former classmate always wore a red and green plaid shirt, corduroy pants, and anti-mosquito rubber boots. It didn't seem to matter to him that it was midsummer and he had to be boiling in that ridiculous outfit.

Sammy spat on the ground. The gesture meant something more than simple rudeness. I think he wanted me to understand that he'd become a man that day.

"I was on patrol tonight," he told me. "With Barragh McBlack."

I looked around at all the men in the pub. "Why you?" I said.

"Someone had to go," he said defensively. "And I know how to use a rifle."

"Were you the one who fired at Mr. Lily, then?" I asked, hoping to catch him off-guard.

Sammy Monkfish laughed. "Are you kidding?" he said. "If it had been me, Mr. Lily would be dead already."

It took everything I had to restrain myself from punching him square in the nose. Instead, I kicked the leg of the stool he sat on.

"Hey!" Sammy cried out as he hit the ground. He sprang to his feet and got right up in my face. "What's your problem, McPhee?! Don't tell me you're on the thief's side."

"The thief?" I said. "Sammy, are you seriously saying that Mr. Lily stole the town's missing sheep?"

Sammy narrowed his eyes. "Of course I am!"

"Then you're an idiot," I said, and entered the pub. There was no point in arguing with Sammy. I had to find someone reasonable to tell what Aiby, Meb, Patches, and I had discovered. I wasn't even planning to tell anyone about Green Jack. No one would believe me. Not yet.

I walked into the pub and kept elbowing through the crowd of people. Judging by the mix of stable smells and fish fumes that hung in the air, the news must have brought everyone to the pub.

The Greenlock had three rooms, a large fireplace, a blackboard with the daily menu (which hadn't changed in over a year), and the bar. As usual, Michael, the son of the owner, towered over the available taps while handing out mug after mug of ale.

"Typical McBlack, huh?" I heard a man say.

"He says he saw Mr. Lily setting a trap with raw meat!" another said.

"Was he alone?"

"No. Another man was with him."

"Wrong. He was alone, I tell you!"

"And when did all this happen?"

"No more than an hour ago."

"Did you hear the shot?"

It was pure chaos. The scene definitely proved that men are every bit as gossipy as old women.

I kept my head down while dodging elbows. Patches snuck through the crowd at my heels. I noticed Reverend Prospero sitting in a corner and having a serious talk with Professor Everett. I headed in their direction, figuring they'd have the best information of the day's

events. Suddenly, a strong hand pulled me out of the crowd.

I turned to see my brother staring at me. "Doug!" I cried.

"Did you hear?" he asked, a concerned look on his face.

I wanted to mock him for his dumb question, but I restrained myself. "Do you know where Locan is?" I asked.

"This way," my brother said. He led me around the bar, toward the bathrooms. He opened a small door at the top of some steps and we entered.

"How is Aiby's father doing?" I asked Doug as we climbed the creaky staircase. My legs felt like bricks due to the long trek earlier that day.

"Barragh shot him in the arm," Doug said. "Nothing too serious, but he lost a lot of blood. However, it's almost a miracle that they were able to carry him as far as they did."

I nodded grimly. Doug pushed open a door and we found ourselves in a long and narrow corridor. On the far end, I heard Aiby's voice. I wanted to run to her.

"We found the lair, Doug," I told my brother. Quickly, I explained to him what we'd discovered that afternoon.

177

"I did what I had to do, you rude little brat!" Barragh McBlack yelled. "I'm sorry for the accident, but your father shouldn't have been sneaking around at night like a common thief!"

"So it's shoot first and ask questions later?!" Aiby shouted.

"Watch your mouth, girl!" Barragh yelled back. "It just so happens that thieves were in my house today, so I was on edge! And if you continue to talk to me like this, we'll keep you here until Bobby Thorne arrives!"

Bobby Thorne was the district's police officer. He didn't live in Applecross, so summoning him meant we had to rely on a person who made a living of avoiding anything difficult. The only reason Bobby could be convinced to come in a timely fashion was for "evidence gathering" on the farms, which really meant begging for slices of blueberry pie from the farmers' wives.

"My father is not the sheep thief!" Aiby yelled at the end of the hall.

"We'll see about that!" Barragh McBlack yelled just as loudly. It occurred to me that I should probably go hide the Sherwood Compass, which was now sitting in the backseat of Meb's car.

Barragh burst out of the room, his mustache quivering. "This isn't over!" he exclaimed.

As he pushed past us, Doug motioned for me to wait. He approached the door where Barragh had just exited. "Can we come in?" he asked.

In response, my father appeared in the doorway. "Dad?" I asked, puzzled.

He seemed equally surprised. He wore a pair of round glasses and was wiping his hands on a towel that had once been white.

"Get that dog out of here, Finley," he ordered. "I don't want Locan getting an infection."

I kneeled to hold Patches back. I knew Dad had studied medicine before he met my mother, and that he'd worked for a few months as a veterinarian's assistant. Even still, I figured he would never be the first choice for treating a gunshot wound. That meant he was the only one to offer help until the real doctor arrived.

"How is Mr. Lily?" I whispered. My dad violently rubbed his hands on his towel, then looked at me as if I were an idiot for asking.

"I removed the bullet," he said. "And I did my best to disinfect the wound. Now we can only wait."

I glanced behind him and saw Mr. Lily lying on a bed. His eyes were closed and his hair was matted on his forehead. He was shirtless and very pale, and his arm was in a crudely wrapped bandage.

"But it's nothing serious . . . right?" I asked.

Aiby appeared in the doorway. She held a hunting bullet in her palm. "My dad has silver bullets in his pocket," she said, and then looked at me. "Do you understand what this means, Finley?"

Aiby's green eyes were on fire. I could tell her teeth were clenched. "Dad was hunting for Green Jack," she said, pointing at the gun next to Locan on the table. "Those bullets wouldn't have killed him, though, which means my dad was going to challenge him. Do you understand? The Green Man came to Applecross to challenge my father to his game. That was his plan." Aiby lowered her voice. "If they hadn't been seen by Barragh McBlack . . . if he hadn't been shot . . . he'd be playing for his life right now."

"Aiby . . ." I began. I just didn't know what to say to her.

"Finley, that gesture you saw the Green Man making," she said. "Do you know what it was?"

I shook my head.

"A deck of cards," Aiby said. "He was shuffling a deck of cards. Green Jack plays for your soul in a game of Black Jack. Twenty-one."

"Twenty-one," I repeated. "Just like the number of peppers in that whiskey bottle."

Aiby nodded. "The same amount of days he stays after being summoned."

And the number of grams a human soul weighs, I thought.

SOUL CARDS

These cards are almost identical to a normal deck of cards except that the face cards are different. Instead of a Jack of Clubs, there's a Dog of Clubs, and instead of a King of Spades, there's a Donkey of Spades, etc. One must possess a Magic Soul in order to play with these cards.

ENCHANTED EMPORIUM

Chapter
NINETEEN

TORCHES,
AN INTRUDER,
& NIGHTMARES

I told our story about Green Jack's lair in the forest and how to reach it three separate times to three different groups of people. Then I watched as countless cars departed. A short time later, I saw torches spreading out across the countryside. And I was scared for them, because this Green Jack was anything but harmless.

Needless to say, I was exhausted when I arrived home well after midnight. I leaned my bicycle against the house and noticed that Dad's van was still gone, which meant he was still out there searching.

I sighed and went upstairs to my room.

I slept for a whole day.

When I finally woke up and went downstairs, it was early evening again. Bobby Thorne was eating a slice of blueberry pie in our living room. My mother was sitting on the opposite edge of the couch, wearing an expression that seemed to mean she'd seen all this coming from a mile away.

"So this is the youngest McPhee!" the cop exclaimed. He wiped his hand on his pants and held it out to me. "You're such a little fella!"

I shook his hand while fantasizing about puncturing the tires on his car. I mean, "little fella" — seriously? *Oh, you adults,* I thought. *You'll never understand anything about anything.*

"Is everything all right, Finley?" my mother asked. She usually didn't let me sleep so much.

My stomach growled. "I'm a little, um, hungry."

She stood. "I'll cook you something."

I thanked her. Only then did I notice the hunched-over figure in the rear corner of the room: my dad. "How is Mr. Lily?" I asked him.

"He still has a high fever, but I think he's going to be fine."

"Is there anyone with him now?"

"Meb stopped by to watch over him."

Mom patted my shoulder and sighed as she passed by

me. "Good thing Meb is there," she said. "The thought of poor Aiby all alone with her dad like that . . ."

"And the other one?" I asked. "The man who was with Mr. Lily, I mean. Did you find him?"

As if remembering he had a job to do, Bobby Thorne set down his crumb-filled plate on the coffee table in front of him. "I think at this point I can leave, Camas. If you hear more news, call me. I'll do the same." He pushed off his knees to stand. "Thanks for the small talk. Magnificent pie, Mrs. McPhee!"

We walked him to the door and watched him climb into his car, turn on his headlights, and leave.

"I'll check on the sheep this time, Doug," my father said in a weary voice. "They haven't been eating lately."

He left, slamming the door behind him. I turned to my brother and asked, "So what happened while I was sleeping?"

My mother and Doug sat with me at the kitchen table and gave me a brief summary of the previous day's events. Mr. Lily had returned home after seeing the real doctor, who arrived from Inverness. "He complimented your father's work on Mr. Lily," Mom said proudly.

"And Dad insisted on sleeping in the village. He refused to come home until Mr. Lily was ready to be moved," my brother added malignantly, which meant he'd had to take care of the farm himself while Dad was gone.

"And what about Green Jack?" I asked.

They glanced at each other, then Doug said, "We searched for him all day. We even went places you didn't tell us to check."

"And?"

"Nothing," Doug said. "No trace, Finley. Meaning . . . we didn't find the sheep or even the cave. Nothing."

"That's impossible!" I said. "I saw it with my own eyes!"

Doug nodded. "Meb came with us, but she couldn't find the cave, either."

We need the compass to find it, I realized. I narrowed my eyes at Doug. "What about Aiby?"

"She's fine," he said.

I yawned again. "You look pale," my mother told me. I quickly finished my dinner and went back upstairs, too dazed to talk anymore. I fell asleep, and dreamt of small, multicolored beetles swarming up through the floorboards of my room.

I don't know how long I slept, but I awoke with a start. I felt lonely there in the darkness, like the shadows in my room were made of roots that wrapped around me.

I tried to take a deep breath, but it felt like I was swallowing a heavy stone.

Patches jumped onto the bed and wagged his tail happily. I ran my fingers through his fur, which made me feel a little better. He nuzzled his head into my armpit.

Slivers of light from my window filtered through the dust in the air. Seagull calls began to fill the morning air. I could hear every sound reverberate on my skin. It was a really strange feeling.

I stood up and set Patches on the floor. Slowly, I left my room. The house was quiet. The lights were off, allowing the white daylight to cast shadows on the walls.

My head down, I washed my hands in the sink for a long time. I couldn't seem to get them clean. I wondered if I'd just gotten tanner, or something.

I grabbed a nearby cup and filled it. As I drank, I felt the water flow down my throat and expand inside me. Then I looked in the mirror.

"What?!" The sight of my reflection blasted away the last of my drowsiness. My eyes were more sunken than usual. My uncombed hair was ratty. And there was something strange on my face. I lifted my fingers to my chin and cheeks.

Finley McPhee has the beginnings of a beard, I realized. I thought it'd be years until I'd have to shave! I don't know

how long I stood in front of that mirror, turning my face to one side and the other, examining my whiskers. But at some point I saw something behind me in the mirror.

I wasn't alone. A second person was in the mirror. And I was certain that if I turned to look behind me, no one would be there.

Despite my confusion, I smiled at the image of my grandma. My father's mother smiled back at me. She looked exactly like I'd remembered her before she'd died after my seventh birthday.

For some reason, I wasn't surprised to see her. I knew I wasn't dreaming. And that meant she wasn't really dead.

"Hello," I said.

The ghost of my grandmother slowly parted her lips. Her mouth was filled with blooming flowers.

"Adele Babele," she said. "Search after Adele Babele." Her voice sounded just like the one I'd been hearing in my head.

"Why should I look for Adele Babele?" I asked, in awe of what was transpiring.

But she'd disappeared. I sighed and rested my hands on the sink. I stared at the point where the pipes met the floor, then raised my eyes to watch the water spiral down

the drain. I imagined it disappearing into the pipes and going underground.

For some reason, the multicolored beetles came to mind. And just like that, as if by magic, I realized what my grandmother had meant.

* * *

I put on my usual pair of jeans, hustled downstairs, and jotted down a note to my parents that said I went to work early at the beach.

I grabbed my backpack and pushed its contents aside so Patches could jump in. "Come on, boy," I said.

As I pedaled my bike toward town, my joints screamed at me. My elbows, knees, shoulders — even my toes were stiff and aching. I figured it must've been because of all the sleep I'd gotten lately.

So I clenched my teeth and pushed the pedals even harder. Sure enough, the pain began to melt away. I felt strange. Very strange.

I felt older.

Chapter
TWENTY

ADELE,
CURIOSITY,
& AN ASKELL

The early morning light painted the white houses of Applecross village a warm gold. The sea slid languidly along the coast, and the tree branches along the road stretched over me like a fishing net. The fields, dotted with sheep, rose gently over the pass like a blanket tucked over the earth. The only sounds that broke the silent dawn were the whirring of my bike and the gentle splash of seagulls diving for fish.

When I arrived at the square, I quietly leaned my bike against the wall just outside the window of The Curious Traveler. I kneeled down to look underneath the table Mr. Everett sat at every day, expecting to find some of the weird beetles I'd seen before, but I saw none.

The strange morning haze made me recall a detail from earlier in the week. I remembered seeing what looked like multicolored insects fall from the hair of that strange lady, Adele Babele. I'd also seen them in this very spot on the day when I'd picked up the strange playing card that fell beneath Professor Everett's table.

The more I thought about it, the more I realized the beetles I'd seen were nothing at all like the black and green varieties we typically had here in Scotland.

That fact made me wonder if Adele Babele had been here too. That's when I remembered the professor had said a new tenant would soon be renting the apartment behind the shop. Was Adele Babele the new tenant he spoke of? If so, what reason would she have to stay in the village?

Aiby said the Flowers of Vertigo would be ready in five days, so maybe Adele changed her mind and chose to stick around until they were finished. But why rent the apartment in the back of Professor Everett's shop instead of getting a room at the McStay Inn?

Those were the questions that occupied my mind, and I was determined to find answers to all of them. I stood in front of the door to the Curious Traveler. I could almost hear my heart leap into my throat in the strange silence of early dawn.

I slowly turned my key and inched open the door. With my senses on high alert, I could even hear Patches' quiet breathing as we entered the shop. I hesitated at the doorstep when a little voice in the back of my head whispered, *Wait.*

"All right, Grandma," I whispered, choosing to listen to her for once. I lingered in the doorway for a few moments. When my hesitation eventually vanished like the dwindling thrill of fear, I went inside.

The shop was silent and dark. I tiptoed through a literal forest of objects attached to strings. Strangely, Professor Everett had hung at least thirty tree-shaped air fresheners from the ceiling. Either he was trying to cover up a bad smell, or his taste in design had taken a turn for the worse.

Just then, I heard a young and animated voice. It had come from the back door, so I pressed my ear up against it. The clear sounds of a conversation filled my ear.

"I'm really very sad that you want to leave," someone said. "I was starting to have so much fun with our great actor."

A chime-like laugh followed. "Oh, my dear Askell! I can always leave him behind, if you like him so much!" The speaker had a bellowing voice. I immediately realized it belonged to Adele Babele.

"No thank you, ma'am! Please take that . . . demon far, far away from me," a man said.

I grabbed the curtain rod at the top of the door and used it to lift myself up so I could see through the window over it. What I saw in the backyard was puzzling to say the least. The fence was open, and a young man in a jogging suit and sneakers had a Cloak of Mirrors draped over his arm. He was talking with Adele Babele, who was leaning out the window of a carriage attached to a pair of inky, black horses. A scarecrow with buttons for eyes was propped up in the coachman's seat, and the Suitcase of Stars was tied to the carriage's rooftop.

Adele Babele leaned back into the carriage and settled herself. "But yes, I must leave soon," she said. "I hope, however, to make the return trip in the company of another dear friend . . . if you know what I mean."

The man nodded. "A deal is a deal, ma'am," he said. "And an Askell —"

"Rarely honors agreements," Adele Babele interrupted with a smirk.

The man half-bowed. "Things have changed," he said.

"How so, young man?" Adele asked. "Besides an Askell running at dawn, I mean."

194

The man shrugged. "Let's just say I've adopted a more modern perspective than my peers, my lady."

"You deny that you live in the past, young Askell," Adele said. "Yet above all else, you wish to take that shabby Enchanted Emporium back from the Lily family."

"A deal is a deal," he repeated. "You get *The Big Book of Magical Objects*, and I get the shop and what's inside it. What each of us shall do with our prizes, well . . . that's none of the other's business."

"That's right," Adele Babele said. She tapped on the carriage. *Poof!* The scarecrow coachman sprang to life! "I'd better go now, or I'll miss my appointment — and the book. I need not remind you that this conversation must remain private, correct?"

The man tilted his head. "You doubt me?" he asked.

"I have doubts about my doubts," she said coyly. "You are unpredictable, Semueld. Perhaps almost as unpredictable as the Green Man who summoned me here."

The man named Semueld snickered. "You summoned him!" he said. "If only that cheating crook would have immediately challenged Locan Lily instead of challenging that poor old fool Cumai first. What a waste of time, terrorizing the poor and feeble. We would have

easily gained a week's time if he'd just gotten right to the important task."

"True," Adele said. "Thankfully, all it took was a little push to get him back on the right track."

"A push, and a few good bottles of whiskey," Semueld said. "If only Barragh McBlack hadn't interrupted our demon's game with Locan Lily . . ."

Adele sighed and nodded. "In any case, it's time for me to leave," she said. "In exactly fifteen minutes, my Rainbow Scarabs will scurry out of the Emporium with the *Big Book of Magical Objects* on their backs. Then my collection will finally be complete. After that, you can do whatever you want with their shabby little shop."

"And then I'll have you to thank, I think," Semueld said.

The carriage began to leave. Adele leaned out the window, and a couple of Rainbow Scarabs fell from her fingers.

"Do not rush things, Mr. Askell," she said. "After yesterday's interruption, I believe our Green Jack will finish his task later this evening. If you linger too long in the village, there is the risk that he will sense your Magic Soul."

"The Others will not be happy," Semueld Askell said.

"Sorry to disappoint you, Askell, but the Others are never happy with us," she said. "Neither you nor I!"

Semueld Askell raised his arm and saluted. Then, when the coach was gone, he turned to the door where I was hiding. His glacial, blue eyes locked onto mine.

"I take it you heard everything?" he asked.

THE SUITCASE OF STARS

Also known as the Wanderers' Burden, the Suitcase of Stars
is actually a type of map. The inside lining contains beadwork
in the shape of the constellations. Individual beads can be
moved to alter the stellar configuration, which teleports
the traveler to the exact place on Earth where an identical
astral copy can be seen at that point in time.

Chapter
TWENTY-ONE

DEAD EYES,
A DEADLY CARD,
& DEATH

Yes I'd heard everything. Every single word. I should have run away mid-conversation. I should've jumped on my bike and gone to warn Aiby that Adele Babele was behind everything and that she planned to steal *The Big Book of Magical Objects*.

Instead, curiosity kept me nailed to the spot. And I had no idea what made me open the door and stand face to face with Semueld Askell in the flesh.

"Who are the Others?" I asked.

He shrugged. "They are the Others," he said. "Those who know the Passing."

"The psychopomps," I said.

His smile froze for a moment, then transformed into a laugh. "I don't believe it," he said. "Have the Lilys been teaching you?" He took a step closer. He was tall with a wiry frame and long, sinewy arms. On his chest was a coat of arms with the letters "I" and "U" in the center.

"What do you want?" I asked him.

Just then, far away, I heard the neighing of a horse. An urgent need to defend the Enchanted Emporium rose within me.

Askell must have heard it too. "What are you waiting for?" he said with a grin. *"The Big Book of Magical Objects* is in danger, and you're just standing here chatting with me?"

"Leave Aiby out of this," I said.

Semueld took a step closer. "Or you'll do what?" he challenged.

I clenched my fists. "Or I'll send you to the other world."

He leaned over me with relentless slowness and a fixed grin. Patches's furious barking could have woken up the whole county.

"Be very careful, McPhee," Semueld Askell said, stressing each syllable. "Being the defender of the Enchanted Emporium is never a safe job . . ."

He lifted his finger and rested it on my temple. As he did, I saw a crack open in his cold right eye. It looked like lightning emerging from within the eye of a storm.

He backed away and slipped his arm into the Cloak of Mirrors. Slowly, he pulled out the *High Voltage* sign that I'd dropped earlier in the week. He opened his palm, releasing the sign. It floated in the air between us.

"Fatal if touched," he whispered, speaking the words like an incantation. The tin-plated sign began to spin like a blade.

"Patches, go!" I called out, running at full speed down the road. All I could think of was reaching my bike as quickly as possible. I heard a whirring sound following me, and I somehow knew that sign he'd thrown would relentlessly pursue whomever had touched it. *Me.*

Patches leaped into my backpack and I jumped onto the saddle. I stood up on the pedals and pushed as hard as I could. The bike raced down the road.

I turned to look behind me. The sign was hissing in pursuit, hovering about eight inches above the ground. I thought of nothing but escape. I took the coastal road toward Reginald Bay, knowing I had to get there before Adele Babele.

Even though I felt stiff, achy, and trapped within my

own body, I pedaled like a madman. My legs pumped with every ounce of strength I had.

I pedaled. And pedaled. My jaw began to hurt from clenching my teeth. I heard the chain whir as it raced over the chain ring's teeth.

I climbed the long hill like it was nothing, left the county, rounded the first and second corners, passed the Cumai mill (and the stream where I loved to go fishing), and kept pedaling down the coastal road.

The pain became almost unbearable, so I distracted myself by thinking about what I had just heard: the agreement to destroy the Lily family, the summoning of Green Jack, and how he searched for Magic Souls and challenged their owners to a game of blackjack. Had he played old lady Cumai, and won? Did that mean she'd had a Magic Soul?

I finally reached the top of the longest climb and launched into the downhill section that separated me from Reginald Bay. I passed through the ridge, still pedaling furiously, and started the long descent toward the bay.

I increased my speed. I saw the first corner a hundred yards ahead at the bottom of the descent. The wind slapped at my cheeks, and I saw the sea sparkling as it scrolled along to my left. I thought back to all the different kinds of beaches down there — the stony ones, the sandy ones, and the one with that giant pile of seaweed . . .

Gasping for breath, I turned around to check if the sign had exhausted its energy yet. Surprisingly, it was no longer following me. I stopped pedaling and allowed myself to coast for a moment as I considered what to tell Aiby when I arrived at the Enchanted Emporium. I wasn't quite sure what to say, since I'd first seen the colored beetles fall from Adele's hair in the shop, but hadn't told Aiby about it because I'd been too worried about my pants.

And then, as if I'd snapped back to reality, I realized I was riding down the road at breakneck speed. The curve was right ahead and I didn't have time to apply the brakes.

I heard the unmistakable notes of *You Can Dance* by ABBA permeate the fresh morning air. Then I saw Jules's red van turning the corner like a red lightning bolt . . . and he was headed right for me.

I knew it would happen eventually. Sooner or later, Jules would run someone over. I just hadn't expected that someone would be me.

Jules didn't even brake. In his defense, there wasn't enough time. He turned the van just enough to avoid hitting me head on, but the side of his van still clipped my bike. Before I knew it, I was airborne.

As Patches and I flew through the air like two clumsy bullets, I realized it was the second time that I'd been airborne that week. I recalled the fall I'd experienced with Locan Lily from the mountains of Shangri-La while searching for the Flowers of Vertigo. I'd fallen through the air for what seemed like an eternity . . .

The incident with Jules didn't last nearly that long. You know how they tell you that when you are about to die, you see your whole life flash before your eyes? Like a movie? Well, the truth is that there wasn't nearly enough time. A mere moment after being thrown from the saddle, I found myself smashing into the beach I had just been thinking about. Luckily, Patches fell on a pile of seaweed and bounced back to his feet like some kind of athletic stuffed animal.

I, however, fell on the stones.

And I died.

Chapter
TWENTY-TWO

DARKNESS,
STILL LIFE,
& A SCRATCH

"Finley? Finley, can you hear me?" It was Aiby. I could hear her quite clearly, but I had no idea how. I couldn't see anything. Rather, there was nothing at all to see.

I was surrounded by darkness. It consumed me. I felt it pressing against my skin.

Where am I? I wondered. *And why do I hear Aiby's voice?* Weirder still, I could hear my thoughts out loud, as if they were spoken.

What the heck is happening? I thought.

Then I saw myself waking up. At dawn. I went into my bathroom and I looked in the mirror. *The beard, Finley,* came a dim voice. *Do you remember when you realized you were growing a beard?*

I remember it, Grandma, I thought.

Think again, my grandmother whispered. *It wasn't a beard. It was something more.*

Great, I thought in the darkness. *The only thing worse than a voice inside your head is a voice inside your head that only speaks in riddles.*

I can't stay for much longer, Finley, my grandma said. *Soon I'll have to leave.*

Where? I thought.

There are many curious things about this side of existence, the voice whispered.

Well now it all makes sense, Grandma, I thought sarcastically.

Enough with the jokes, Finley, Grandma said. *Time to wake up!*

I don't want to "wake up," I thought. *I want to stay here with you.*

But it didn't really feel like a choice. I wondered if I really did make my own choices, or if something else just told me what to do all the time. Could I choose for myself?

Not this time, came her soft voice. And then Grandma left me.

"Finley, please . . . can you open your eyes?" I knew that voice, too.

Only one way to find out, I thought.

So I opened my eyes. There was Aiby. She was beneath me somehow. I watched her from above, as if I had grown to an enormous size, or like she'd become much smaller. But she was still the Aiby I knew, tall and thin, and gesturing with her hands every time she spoke.

We were on a beach. In fact, I recognized it as Beach #8, the one with the seaweed pile.

"Can you see me?" Aiby asked.

"Yes I see you," I said. "What are you doing way down there?"

"How are you?" she asked.

How am I? I wondered. I didn't really know yet. "Achy," I replied. "Super sore." I tried to move, but couldn't.

She nodded gravely. "Stay still, if you can," she said. "I think it's better if you don't move."

"Agreed," I said. "I think I've been in an accident."

I saw movement, and realized that it wasn't just me and her on the beach. Mr. Lily, pale as a ghost and with a bandaged arm, was leaning on Meb. My brother was right behind them. I didn't understand what they were doing here and why they all seemed so far away.

"Aiby," I said. "What's going on?"

She hugged me. This time, it felt completely different.

It was like she wasn't really embracing me. I didn't feel her body close to mine, like before. I felt something different and deeper that made my feet tingle.

"It's okay, Finley," she said. "It's all right."

"The book!" I cried. "Adele Babele has hidden her tiny beetle thieves inside the shop and . . ."

She hugged me even tighter. "Yes, Finley," she said. "We discovered it."

"And how did you do that?" I asked.

"It was Jules," she said. "After he hit you, he drove back to the shop and got there just as Adele's carriage arrived. He honked wildly and Meb and I rushed out, catching her — and her beetles — in the act."

"Did you get the book back?" I asked.

"Sure did!" she said. "It's safe inside the Enchanted Emporium. You don't have to worry about that now."

I nodded. Or, rather, I tried to nod. "I met Semueld Askell, and . . ."

I had to stop. It was too hard to talk and breathe at the same time. I felt like my lungs were filled with moss.

"Don't worry about Semueld Askell," she said. "Now that you're awake, we'll take care of everything. You'll see. Have faith in me."

I don't know why, but I didn't believe her one bit. Her voice just seemed wrong, like she was speaking to

a child. She wouldn't be talking to me like that if she'd seen my beard. She didn't understand that I was growing up.

I noticed that the other people on the beach were peering at me in a strange way, like I was on TV . . . or in a hospital bed. "Why is Meb crying?" I asked.

Aiby turned to look at Meb. Then, without answering me, she took a deep breath and said, "Now listen, Finley. You remember that you had a bad accident, right?"

"Of course," I said. "Wait — is Patches okay?!"

Right on cue, my trusty friend trotted to Aiby's side. But just like her, Patches seemed to be terribly far away.

"Oh, good. And my bike?" I asked.

"We'll fix it," Aiby said. You could tell she wanted to talk about something else, but she hesitated.

"Do you want to explain to me once and for all what the situation is?" I asked. "A moment ago, I thought I was dead."

Aiby smiled. "Well, you know . . . the accident you were in would have killed pretty much anyone."

"You underestimate me, Aiby," I said. "You always do."

"Really?" she asked. "Then I'll ask you again: did you read the description of the Sherwood Compass?"

A knot grew in my stomach. "Yes. So?"

Aiby tilted her head. "Then you remember it all?" she asked.

I hesitated.

She crossed her arms. "Like when it said to be very careful with the tip of the weather vane?" she asked. "And to make absolutely certain it didn't cut anyone?"

I thought for less than a second. "No," I admitted.

Aiby grunted. "Of course not. Otherwise, you would've known that the tip of the weather vane was coated with the Lifeblood of the Forest. That's what gives it the power of divination."

"Go on," I whispered, visualizing the scrape I'd gotten from the vane.

"If you're cut by the point," she added, "then the Lifeblood of the Forest is . . . mixed with yours."

I felt numb panic set in. "So what does that mean?" I asked.

Aiby hesitated. "It means . . . you are now a Green Man."

"Huh?" I asked. "What do you mean I'm a Green Man?"

I thought about all the discomfort I'd felt recently. When I was using the Sherwood Compass, the fatigue and stiffness while biking, my dirty and slightly green hands . . .

I tried to look at myself and realized I couldn't. I was completely paralyzed. I could see only a little of what was in front of me.

"To be honest with you, Finley," Aiby murmured, "the Lifeblood of the Forest saved your life . . . by turning you into a tree."

Chapter
TWENTY-THREE

TEARS,
LAUGHTER,
& DREAMING

It took a while to think of a response. "And now what should I do?" I said. I wagged my little branches in frustration.

Aiby laughed at my gesture. Then she bit her lip and nodded at the others. They moved closer.

"Hey, Doug," I said. "Did you take my photo already?"

"You bet."

"How do I look?" I asked.

"Honestly?" he said. "Kind of awesome."

I looked at Aiby's dad. "Mr. Lily, it's nice to see you're up and about again," I said. "So what's the plan?"

He looked at Aiby, and she spoke to me instead. "Our idea is to . . . well, you see, the process of transforming

into a Green Man occurred at the very moment when you had the accident. The adrenaline in your body reacted with the sap in your blood, and —"

"Listen, Aiby," I interrupted. "I know your plan will be perfect, but I don't think I can handle hearing an explanation right now."

"And the process keeps going," Mr. Lily added. I saw he was holding himself up by Meb's shoulder. "So it is possible that, at any moment, you'll no longer be able to see, speak, or even hear us anymore."

"Great," I said.

Meb wailed. She was taking this harder than I was. "Hey Meb, I gotta ask," I said. "What kind of tree am I?"

"You look like an oak tree," Meb said between sniffles. "But your, um . . . your trunk is completely white."

"Wow. Not bad, huh?" I said.

Meb laughed. Then she started to cry again.

Aiby placed her palm on my roots. "There is only one thing we can try to do to stop the process and reverse it. I need to inject you with a golden needle filled with the Water of Dreams."

"Dream water, huh," I said. "What's that do?"

"It's a distilled, crystalline water. It's very rare and extremely valuable. And it is capable of purifying almost

anything. I believe it . . . well, it *might* cancel the effect of the sap and return you to normal."

I scanned their faces, one by one. They all seemed worried. "And why do you say *might*?"

"The Water of Dreams is highly unstable," Mr. Lily said. "It works on the subconscious through one's dreams, and allows for miraculous healing if pleasant dreams are had." He bit his lip. "But if the dreams are bad, or unclear, it doesn't have any effect."

"So, what you're saying is that it's all up to me if it works or not?"

Aiby touched my trunk. "To go back, you need to *want* to go back. That's all. You have to think of someone or something that is important to you. Think of a happy moment in your life, and how your body felt and looked at that time. You have to visualize it, and it must be from before the point when you scraped yourself with the compass. If you dream clearly of that moment, then the Water of Dreams will allow you to return to that form."

"Okay," I replied. "That sounds easy enough."

Aiby shook her head. "It's not easy," she said. "No one knows how to control their dreams."

"You're wrong," I said. "Come on, let's do this."

Aiby hesitated. "Are you sure?"

"Do I have any alternatives?" I asked.

Mr. Lily turned to Meb. She produced a giant, golden syringe from her bag. It looked more like a fencer's foil than a medical tool.

"No way!" I screamed. "I'd rather stay a tree than let you stab me with that thing!"

"Finley!" Doug scolded. "Don't be such a baby."

"I've always hated needles!" I cried. "You know that."

"But you're a tree!" he said.

"So?" I said. "Why don't you go turn yourself into a tree and then maybe you can tell me it's no big deal to get stabbed by that thing!"

A cold wind blew in from the sea, ruffling my leaves. A seagull landed on one of my branches. I eyed it warily.

"Okay, fine," I said. "Let's just get on with the stabbing, Meb."

Meb knelt in front of me. Carefully, she injected me with the Water of Dreams just above the roots. I felt a tingling sensation — and then nothing.

"You didn't rub it with a cotton ball first," I said. "What if I get an infection or something?"

She laughed. Then she looked at me strangely and said, "Don't make jokes, Finley."

"So now what?" I asked.

"Now you dream," whispered Aiby's father. And I realized that it was no longer morning, but nearing

dusk. "We'll leave you alone now, because the Water of Dreams only works in solitude. We'll come back tomorrow at dawn. And everything will be all right, Finley."

What about my parents? I thought.

Seemingly reading my mind, Doug said, "Don't worry about Mom and Dad. I'll come up with an excuse for you."

Doug took a few steps back, then turned to help Meb guide Mr. Lily to the car. Aiby, however, remained on the beach. She said nothing for a long time, watching the waves wash over her feet. Eventually, she hugged me and pressed her face against my white bark.

I wanted to say something meaningful to her. Something philosophical, or deep. But I couldn't think of anything, so I just kept quiet.

Aiby let me go. "I know you can do it, Finley," she said.

"You've always underestimated me," I reminded her.

She smiled. "No," my best friend said. "I never did." Then she planted a kiss on my trunk. Tree or not, I shivered.

Doug came over and gave me a punch on the trunk. "Don't be long, okay?" he said. "When I said I'd break you in half, I didn't mean like firewood."

I shook my biggest limbs in laughter. "Good one," I said. "And don't worry, bro. Tomorrow morning I'll be good ol' Viper again."

"I know," he said. "I'll leave you some clothes to change into when you're back to normal, okay? No one wants to see you naked."

He laid a pair of pants on the beach over my roots, then set a few stones on top of them so they wouldn't blow away. "I got those jeans you said you liked. Remember?"

I had no idea what he was talking about, but I appreciated the gesture. "Oh, yes. Thanks, Doug."

Doug frowned, then slipped off his rugby shirt — the one he wore during games. His lucky jersey. "Here," he said in a cracked voice. "You get any blood or sap or whatever on this and you're dead meat."

At that moment, I realized trees couldn't cry, but they can change the color of their trunks to a darker shade. At least I could, anyway. I rustled my smaller branches, hoping Doug would understand that his gesture meant a lot to me.

Doug nodded, then left with his hands shoved in his pockets. Patches whined on the ground, rubbing his nose against my trunk. Before he left, he wished me good luck by peeing on my roots.

★ ★ ★

Night came. I was alone, just as I had been before.

I looked out at the moonlit waves of the sea. I felt a tingling all over my skin — err, my bark — like I was giving off steam. I realized that I was slowly drifting to sleep.

I had to think about myself, like Aiby told me. Something about me or my life that made it feel worthwhile to go back to being Finley McPhee instead of a tree.

It was a tough task, since I had a million good memories of all kinds. I wanted to go back to being the Finley who went fishing with Patches. The Finley who loved to watch his brother play rugby but didn't know how to tell Doug that.

I wanted to be the Finley who became an ancient hero in order to defend the Enchanted Emporium from a giant made of stone. The Finley who hugged Aiby near the cliff the other day. I focused on how I felt at the moment we touched. I was alive in every sense of the word.

My thoughts swirled inside me like insects. I could hear them moving, slow and heavy, and I realized that trees had a very different way of thinking. It was more calm and thoughtful, like moving ideas as if they were

physical objects. Important ideas traveled down to the roots in search of nourishment. Other thoughts branched out to sprout and grow, while the more complete ideas seemed to melt in the wind. But ideas never mixed. Instead, each idea remained single and indivisible, like seeds waiting to sprout.

My mother once told me, "Finley, you think about too many things at once." And she was right, I'd always been guilty of that.

Even our superintendent, the Widow Rozencratz, told me as much when she ratted me out to my parents for skipping school to go fishing. I recalled my classmates, like Sammy Monkfish and his notebook scrawled with cuss words. I remembered our fight in front of the pub over the night patrols and the hunt for Green Jack.

And now I was a Green Man. Would Sammy have shot me?

I thought of Semueld Askell and his deadly flying sign.

I thought of the Water of Dreams that flowed through my veins.

I thought about the possibility that I was already dreaming, like in one of those lucid dreams where you realize you're dreaming but can't do anything about it.

I thought of my roots and how they tethered me to the ground. I hated feeling trapped like this. *Paralyzed.*

Then again, being forced to stand still for so long had its advantages. For one thing, I could think more clearly and easily. And it was kind of nice to have some time to just think. I began to wonder what my life would be like as a tree. The idea of only being able to see one fixed point for the rest of my life scared me.

But in a way, it's the same as being human, I realized. *We need a fixed point, too — it's just harder to see sometimes.*

Who am I? I thought. *Well, I'm Finley — with an "F."*

I smiled in my dream. Finley McPhee had always been a likeable goofball, a slacker, and sometimes a liar and a cheater. He loved things like fishing far more than going to school, and because of that fact, he'd probably never learn how to read the Enchanted Language or how to write an Incantation.

I was all these things, but also none of them. I knew, deep down, that I had one fixed point deep within me.

A long time passed in dreams. Then something happened: I saw many small Finleys standing before me. One, two, three . . . seven Finleys in all, all of them the same, yet each one was different. In that moment, I saw myself more clearly than ever before.

I know who I am, I thought. *I've decided.*

I smiled, and my larger limbs rustled just like they had when I'd laughed.

I kept my eyes on the soft warmth of the dreamy sun.

And when I awoke, it was morning.

HOUSER & GRIMES

THE **WATER** OF **DREAMS**

IMPORTERS AND EXPORTERS

The monks of the Himalayan mountains create the Water of Dreams by using mystical techniques to squeeze it from metamorphic rock crystals. The monks then use the liquid during meditation in one of two ways. In small, daily amounts, the liquid helps the user find the Real Self, or recognize one's true desires. With a large, single dosage, it has the potential to miraculously heal an afflicted soul . . . but only if the imbiber's dreams cooperate.

Chapter
TWENTY-FOUR

ONE BROTHER,
TWO BIKES,
& THREE ACES

The next day, I called Doug into my room. "Doug, I just remembered a dream I had a while I was a tree!"

I was lying on my bed on my stomach because it still hurt to sit where Meb had given me the injection. Who would've guessed a tree's roots are located where a human's butt is?

My brother pulled off his headphones. "What dream?" he asked. For a moment, I felt the horrible sound of an electric guitar in my bones.

"I dreamed of a man sneaking through the forest," I said. "He was dressed in colorful clothes, had long hair, and smelled like bellybutton lint. And he was wearing a pair of sunglasses with one broken lens."

"Oh, come on," Doug said, scoffing. "You dreamed of the Green Man?"

"Yes," I said. "Of Green Jack."

I propped myself up on my elbows. "He had his deck of Soul Cards with him, and I knew he wanted to challenge me. The first thing he said was, 'Do you know how heavy the soul is, boy?' And I replied, 'It weighs twenty-one grams.'"

"What did he say back?" Doug asked.

"He nodded and chuckled, then he told me that the weight would be exactly twenty-one grams and that right there was the fun part. Then he shuffled the cards and said, 'Let's do this. Me against you. If you win, you can have your soul back. If I win, I'll take it to the other side. Agreed?' And without waiting for my answer, he dealt me the first card."

"What did you play?" Doug asked.

"Twenty-one, of course," I replied, with a smile. "Do you know how to play?"

"Yes," he told me. "You keep taking cards, trying to get as close as possible to twenty-one without going over. The ace is worth one or eleven, the face cards ten each, and other cards are worth the number written on them."

I nodded. "My first card was an ace."

"And what did you do?" Doug asked.

"I said, 'Hit me.'"

Doug nodded. "And?"

"I got an eight."

"So, an eight and an eleven from the ace gave you nineteen," concluded my brother. "I hope you stayed."

"I asked for another card, Doug."

He shook his head and smirked. "Idiot," he said.

I raised an eyebrow. "And he dealt me another ace."

"No way!" Doug said. "Did your hand beat his?"

I looked at him for a long moment. "Then I asked for another card."

Doug just stared at me blankly.

"And I got the third ace," I said. "Three aces and an eight. Twenty-one. Blackjack."

My brother broke into laughter. "You're crazy, Viper."

"That's what Green Jack said, too!" I said. "He laughed and gathered up the cards without letting me see his hand. Then he whistled, and said, 'That old hag Adele was right when she said I wouldn't be bored in this town. That was a good game, Finley McPhee. A really good game. I haven't lost a hand in ages.' Then he smirked, and added, 'But don't worry, I think we'll play again someday.'"

"Then what happened?"

I shrugged. "Then I woke up on the beach. I barely

had the strength to get dressed before you and Meb arrived and helped me get home."

He grinned. "You know, if you keep sleeping all day, Mom's going to start to get suspicious."

I nodded. "Hey, Doug?"

"What?"

"Here under the bed," I said. "There should be a book . . ."

Doug smirked. He reached under the bed, grabbed the book, and set it next to me on the bed. It was *The Black Book of the Woods*, which I had brought home the night Aiby's dad was shot.

"So you finally want to start learning this stuff, huh, Viper?"

I hesitated. "No. I want you to take it."

Doug heard a noise and went to the window. "Oh, great!" he said. "They're here. Let's go!"

I gestured for him to wait, but he didn't care. I managed to sneak a peek out the window before he tossed me over his shoulder and carried me downstairs and outside.

When Doug set me down, Patches started bounding around my feet in the grass while yipping excitedly. Dad was out working in the fields, but the noise from the tractor was comforting. Mom came up and gave me a cup of coffee and milk without asking any questions. Even though she hadn't forced me to explain my absence the night before, I could tell she was worried.

"Hey Mom," I said. "Do you happen to know where the McBlacks are originally from?"

"Suffolk," she said. "Why?"

I smiled. "No reason," I said. She ruffled my hair and went back inside.

Doug tapped me on the shoulder, then pointed to my right. Next to the front door were two gleaming bicycles, one red and one slightly larger white one!

"Wow!" I said, limping over to them. "Where did these come from?!"

"It doesn't matter," he said. "Do you like them?"

"They're awesome, Doug!" I cried. "But how did you —"

He put me in a headlock and rubbed his knuckles against my scalp.

I grinned and elbowed him off me. Then I looked at the red bike and titled my head. It was missing a fairly important part. "So, um . . . where's the saddle?" I asked.

He chuckled. "Right there."

"Huh?"

Doug put a hand on the frame where bikes normally have saddles. His hand traced a shape. "It's a special, invisible, *magical* saddle," he said, unnecessarily building it up. "Aiby and Locan ordered it. You know, as a welcome back gift."

I was so happy that I almost squealed. I looked up at the clear sky and the islands across the bay, and decided I'd made the right choice to return to normal.

"You should take it for a spin," he said.

"Not now," I said, patting my new bike. "Well, maybe I'll give it a try. There is something I need to take care of today . . ."

I looked out at the sea toward the island where Scary Villa was located. Doug glanced out with me. "Do you want me to come with you?" he asked uncertainly.

I stared at him, struggling to hide my amazement. He pretty much never wanted to do anything with me. "Next time," I said. "I should probably do this alone."

Doug seemed to be relieved. He jerked his thumb over his shoulder. "Then I'm going to go help Dad in the fields." We bumped fists, then he left.

I ran upstairs to my room and stuffed a few things into my backpack. Then I sprinted back downstairs to my new bike.

I gingerly climbed onto the saddle, expecting it to hurt, but was pleasantly surprised to feel like my butt was floating on a cloud.

I'm really going to have to thank the Lilys for this, I thought.

Patches barked. "Sorry, buddy," I said, beginning to pedal away. "You gotta stay behind this time."

Chapter
TWENTY-FIVE

DREAMS,
PROMISES,
& ME

I calmly pedaled to the Dogberry farm, then slowly and carefully loaded my new bike into the boat and pushed it into the water, headed for Scary Villa.

About an hour later, I was standing in front of the gate. I pulled the chain to open it and quickly squeezed through the opening with my bike.

Almost immediately, I heard Cromwell barking. I tensed. It would've been nice to have Patches with me, but he might've gotten hurt. To calm myself, I recalled the last few days' crazy events.

My first trip to Scary Villa. Playing cards with Green Jack. Semueld Askell and the High Voltage sign. Adele Babele and her scarecrow coachman.

Not too long ago, it all would've seemed ridiculous. But now I knew better. Magic did exist. And even if it didn't, it'd be necessary to create it.

While a magical object had helped return me to normal after a brief experience as a tree, it wasn't the Water of Dreams that had actually restored me. Water was just water. But dreams . . . well, dreams showed me the way back home. Back to myself.

"Like a compass," I said to myself. "A compass of dreams."

Aiby was also my compass. Her face seemed so familiar to me despite the fact that I'd only known her for a short time. Yet she too showed me the way.

I walked toward the pointed roof of Scary Villa and passed through the creepy garden statues. "Don't be afraid," I said to myself. "I'm not doing anything wrong. I'm here to do something *right*."

Up until very recently, a little voice inside my head had been speaking to me. It had counseled me and protected me. But now that soft voice was gone, replaced by my own.

Grandma was gone. And I was growing up.

"Lucky her," I said, seeing Cromwell jog into view, every bit as shaggy, ugly, and terrible as before.

Behind Cromwell, I saw the creeping ivy on the villa's walls. My eyes followed it up to the window where I'd seen that girl before. I wondered if she was lonely. If she wanted to talk to someone who wouldn't be scared of her statues. Someone trustworthy.

But what would we talk about? I wondered. Then I smiled. *Perhaps a little, green girl who'd walked through a cave and found herself in a strange forest in Suffolk.*

It hadn't taken me long to put two and two together. In *The Black Book of the Woods*, the little girl in the story was also named Somerled. To confirm my suspicions, I'd asked my mother where the McBlacks were originally from. When she told me they were from Suffolk, I knew my hunch was right.

And so they'd kept her hidden for all those years here inside Scary Villa. It also explained why they'd stolen the Sherwood Compass. After all, it was the only magical item that could track down a Green Person.

So, I continued walking, very slowly, with the Compass Sherwood tucked under my arm. Cromwell sat down and let me pass. It was like he recognized me.

I felt like me. The *real* me. The me I'd dreamed of. The me I'd chosen. The true Finley McPhee.

The one who keeps his promises.

PIERDOMENICO BACCALARIO

I was born on March 6, 1974, in Acqui Terme, a small and beautiful town of Piedmont, Italy. I grew up with my three dogs, my black bicycle, and Andrea, a special girl who lived five miles uphill from my house.

During my boring high school classes, I often pretended to take notes while I actually wrote stories. Around that time, I also met a group of friends who were fans of role-playing games. Together, we invented and explored dozens of fantastic worlds. I was always a curious but quiet explorer.

While attending law school, I won an award for my novel, *The Road Warrior*. It was one of the most beautiful days of my entire life. From that moment on, I wrote and published my novels. After graduating, I worked in museums and regaled visitors with interesting stories about all the dusty, old objects housed within.

Soon after, I started traveling. I visited Celle Ligure, Pisa, Rome, Verona, London, and many other places. I've always loved seeing new places and discovering new cultures, even if I always end up back where I started.

There is one particular place that I love to visit: in the Susa Valley, there's a tree you can climb that will let you see the most magnificent landscape on the entire planet. If you don't mind long walks, I will gladly tell you how to get there . . . as long as you promise to keep it a secret.

IACOPO BRUNO

I once had a very special friend who had everything he could possibly want. You see, ever since we were kids, he owned a magical pencil with two perfectly sharp ends. Whenever my friend wanted something, he drew it — and it came to life!

Once, he drew a spaceship — and we boarded it and went on a nice little tour around the galaxy.

Another time, he drew a sparkling red plane that was very similar to the Red Baron's, only a little smaller. He piloted us inside a giant volcano that had erupted only an hour earlier.

Whenever my friend was tired, he drew a big bed. We dreamed through the night until the morning light shone through the drawn shades.

This great friend of mine eventually moved to China . . . but he left his magic pencil with me!

ENCHANTED EMPORIUM

ENCHANTED EMPORIUM

Come In WE'RE OPEN

SCARSELLI I MAGNIFICI

FIRENZE · BUENOS AIRES

DAL · 1571

Borgo San Jacopo 9/c · Diagonal Norte 615